About the Author

Philip Hurst has written and published two novels: *Prescription for Greed* published by Frederic C. Beil, and *Tarnished* published by Longstreet Press. Dr. Hurst received his Ph.D. in behavioral psychology from Auburn University. He has over twenty years of experience as an international organizational consultant, speaker, and presenter.

Wolf Moon Rising

Philip W. Hurst

Wolf Moon Rising

Vanguard Press

VANGUARD PAPERBACK

© Copyright 2024
Philip Hurst

The right of Philip Hurst to be identified as the author of
this work has been asserted by him in accordance with the
Copyright, Designs and Patents Act 1988.

All Rights Reserved

No reproduction, copy, or transmission of this publication
may be made without written permission.
No paragraph of this publication may be reproduced,
copied or transmitted save with the written permission of the publisher, or in
accordance with the provisions
of the Copyright Act 1956 (as amended).

Any person who commits any unauthorized act in relation to this publication
may be liable to criminal prosecution and civil claims for damages.

A CIP catalog record for this title is available from the British Library.

ISBN 978-1-83794-468-2

This is a work of fiction. Names, characters, businesses, places, events, and incidents are either the products of the author's imagination or used in a fictitious manner. Any resemblance to actual persons, living or dead, or actual events is purely coincidental.

Vanguard Press is an imprint of
Pegasus Elliot Mackenzie Publishers Ltd.
www.pegasuspublishers.com

First Published in 2024

Vanguard Press
Sheraton House Castle Park
Cambridge England

Printed and Bound in Great Britain

Dedication

To my wife, Tamara, family, and friends.

Acknowledgments

I want to thank my good friends, Rachel, Kathy, Glenn, Peggy, Tammy, Leslie, John, and David, who inspired me to keep writing. A special call-out to Craig Langford, who spent countless hours working with me on every word.

Prologue
1780
Comanche Land
A Fool's Dream

Not the slightest whisper of a breeze. A scary stillness across the land. A deadness matched only by the blistering heat from the plains of the Texas Panhandle.

There are few places to hide from the bright, brilliant rays of the sun burning down from a cloudless sky. Not even in the canyons, where you can find an occasional lip of shade from a rock formation, can you escape the rising heat? Looking across the desert is like looking above a blazing fire, all wavy and distorted.

Laying still as a stone with thirty of your finest warriors on a small, concave canyon floor in the middle of summer is no easy task. One sound, one stretch of the neck too high, and the enemy scouts could spot you. The murderous sun tortured your skin, and then there were the insects; fiddleback and black widow spiders, scorpions, fire ants, wasps, and bees. Even worse were the snakes, the venomous rattlesnakes that blended into the terrain were the most feared. It took a person full of hate and discipline to wait completely motionless as a band of Apache slowly meandered over the prairie, hunting for buffalo.

For over a hundred years, the Comanche had been pushing out the Apache, Jumano, and even some Pueblo from this land. Yuma, the Comanche name meaning chiefs' son, had been lucky over the last few weeks and had already led a great hunt; now it was about to get even better. He and his men had tracked a band of Apache, their most hated and fiercest enemy, for most of the day and now lay in ambush as they got closer and closer. Yes, killing them will bring the greatest of war honors. His father would be proud when he brought back fine scalps and handsome horses. He only wished there were women to take as slaves.

When Yuma's father, Muraco, meaning white moon, was young, he was one of the most celebrated warriors in the Comanche nation. The various tribes, from New Mexico to Oklahoma to Texas, had heard of his great fighting skills and wartime leadership. Muraco was known for his accuracy with a bow and arrow, while riding at full gallop, tucked under his horse's neck. Unlike his son, Muraco was strong, tall, and carried a broad chest. You could tell from a distance that this man was unyielding and powerful.

Yuma carried no obvious physical advantages. He was wry and a bit short, but he did have a strong spirit. His childhood name reflected this wildfire spirit. He was called Nayati; he wrestles. But, to his father's great disappointment, he could never win the big tournaments of his tribe. Comanche changed their name with the different phases of their lives to capture their spirit, and he wanted to follow in his father's footsteps and be chief when his father could no longer lead. Yuma often prayed to the Big Father, the creator god, for guidance, and often talked to the animals in the hope that their spirits would continue to protect him in battles. It seemed like no matter how hard Yuma tried, his father seemed disappointed in him and never acknowledged his skills or victories.

The Apache were getting near now. Yuma could hear their horses galloping closer. He could almost taste their blood as he looked at his band of motionless warriors. They were waiting for his signal, a simple war cry that would start the battle. First, they would shoot a hail of arrows. Then, they would foot-charge with their lances and stone tomahawks. The battle would be over within minutes, and the young warriors holding the Comanche horses safely out of sight around a rock formation would soon arrive. Any Apache that turned and ran would be tracked down by Yuma while his warriors gathered the enemy horses that had survived.

The plan was almost picture-perfect. The arrows did their job. A good half of the Apache twenty-man party was seriously hit. During the confusion, the foot charge was quick and brutal. The lances were not thrown like javelins, but were used to stab their enemy from a good six feet away. Once the Apache were off their horses, it was furious and bloody hand-to-hand combat. War clubs smashed skulls. Tomahawks split off limbs. Knives were stuck in Apache's guts and ripped upward.

When the dust settled, all the enemies but one were killed. None escaped. Only two Comanche were killed; Yuma could accept the death toll. His Comanche brothers had died for a good cause. Only three enemy horses were lost. The Comanche were quick to start scalping and carefully tying the scalps to their lances. They would hold their lances high when they arrived home to show off their admirable conquest.

The celebration, however, was short-lived. To the south, a rider was at full gallop, dust chasing from behind. Yuma cupped his hand above his eyes to cut the sun's glare. The Comanche were known for their horse-riding ability. Yuma relaxed as he studied the rider. The mere way he was arched on his horse, holding a bow, told Yuma the rider had to be Comanche.

"Yuma," a warrior called out as he brought the live Apache forward and threw him on the ground, "what shall we do with him?"

There were two choices. Either smash his brains out or cut the top of his skull off and eat his tasty brains while he was alive. The horror on the faces of those chosen for cannibalism and their inevitable begging to die was something Yuma never enjoyed, but it was necessary. The Apache will soon come looking for their hunting party and find their remains. Nothing puts fear in the hearts of their enemies more than to find a body that had been cannibalized.

"Yuma... Yuma..." the rider was shouting as he approached. It was Paco, meaning eagle. He dove off his sweaty horse and grabbed Yuma. "It is your father." His eyes met Yuma's, and, in that instant, Yuma knew what Paco would say, "I am sorry, Yuma. Your father is dead."

Yuma felt pain run through his body. "How?"

"We are not sure. A maiden was taking him water and found him in his tepee motionless. He had been taking a nap after eating."

The others watched Yuma as he strutted and fretted, clenching his teeth. He saw the half-beaten Apache still on his knees. Yuma pulled out his war club and gave a powerful blow to the temple of his enemy. The Apache fell immediately to the ground, head smashed. Yuma began to beat the Apache's head repeatedly. Blood splattered all over him and the dead body. Splinters of the skull were thrown airborne. The others did nothing but watch until the Apache's head had been torn to bits and pieces so badly that Yuma was merely beating the flesh into the ground.

*

Yuma rode hard back to camp, leaving the others behind until he arrived at his father's tepee. When he entered, Yuma saw his mother and sister mourning Muraco's body. The medicine man was waving a feather over him and chanting songs of death. Incense smoke filled the tepee.

Yuma approached the medicine man and pointed for him to move away. Pulling back a buffalo hide covering his father, Yuma studied the still body. There were hundreds of small, sharply raised, round, and firm bumps, like a hard pea under the skin. Most had been broken and scabbed over. He turned to the medicine man and asked, "What has happened to my father?"

The medicine man shook his head with remorse and spoke softly. "Many in the tribe have the same signs as Muraco."

For the entirety of the next day, Yuma pondered his father's strange illness as they prepared for the funeral. Tradition called for Muraco's favorite horse to be killed and buried with him. This would help the great chief ride into the spirit world.

*

After the funeral, the medicine man sent Yuma on a vision quest. He was allowed to gather a few items: a buffalo robe, a bone pipe, some peyote, material to produce fire, and a pouch of water. Yuma knew it was time; he needed to restore his spiritual power. If he was lucky and the vision quest was successful, his guardian spirit would reveal himself to him. After gathering what he needed, Yuma headed out on foot to find an isolated spot. He would fast for four days and smoke peyote three times a day.

He walked south for many miles and stopped when he found a hill that overlooked miles of flat land. There was a large rock shelf that provided plenty of shade. This was a perfect spot for a vision quest. He could see anyone approaching,

On the third day of his quest, he could feel his stomach screaming, but Yuma ignored his need for food, as it would spoil his quest. As the sun rose, he began smoking the harsh peyote. He coughed in convulsions as he inhaled the dense smoke. He felt the cosmic energy starting to slam against his forebrain. Yuma inhaled deeply, knowing that his vision quest had begun.

*

The trees near him began to whisper, "Leave, Yuma… leave, Yuma… death is near."

He shouted back at them, "I am here to see my spiritual guardian. I request a power beyond this world."

The peyote's power continued to increase until a brilliant, bright light was shining on him. He approached the light, but when he turned, he saw his own body sitting up rigidly with his palms pointing to the sky. He walked closer to the light. "Is that you, spirit?"

There was no reply, only the trees whispering, "Leave, Yuma…"

As he stepped forward, he saw a rattlesnake shaking its rattle, close enough to strike. The frightening rattle got more intense. Yuma was now encircled by rattlers. There was only one path he could take to escape as the trees began to chant, "Run, Yuma, run." Instead, Yuma looked each snake in the eye and then sat down.

The snakes tightened the circle and coiled. They were less than five feet away. The one in front of him came forward, hissing and whispering, "You are no Muraco. I sense your fear. I sense your insecurities. Your spirit is weak." The snake came closer and coiled, ready to strike.

Yuma half closed his eyes and began to breathe slowly, inhaling deeply, and then expelling it with a hard exhale. "Go away. I fear you not."

When he opened his eyes, the snake in front of him suddenly struck Yuma's throat. But it was as if the snake dove into a small black hole, into the ether spiritual world, and disappeared instead of striking him. Yuma watched as the other snakes seemed to melt into the ground. It was a test by his guardian spirit to see if Yuma was worthy. A sphere of vibrant, flashing light appeared. "What do you seek?"

"Spiritual power; my tribe is ill and dying." Yuma slowly stood and approached the light. "There are many of all ages that are dying with spots all over their bodies."

The guardian asked again, "What do you seek?"

Yuma didn't hesitate. "Wisdom. To see. To understand."

With that, a portion of the sphere's white light flew at Yuma's face. It slammed into his consciousness like a sledgehammer. He fell to the ground, and when he looked up, the guardian was gone. Looking around, he realized he had his own sphere encompassing him. Unlike the guardian's sphere, he had three distinct colors. Most of the outer shell was green with what looked like two encompassing belts, one blue and one red. As he rested his eyes on the green, he felt a sense of harmony and balance.

The longer he gazed into the green shell, the more revitalized he felt. He shifted his attention to the red and immediately felt the radiance of strong energy. And when he turned his attention and looked at the blue belt, he felt the need to be unique and had a strong sense of compassion.

Then, like watching a movie, he saw his father. His shell was bright yellow, which radiated his intelligence, imagination, and idealism. As his father walked across the rocky landscape, he left a trail of yellow dust like little stars shooting across the sky.

"Father," Yuma called out, but the chief didn't turn toward him. So, he instead followed Muraco over to a campfire where his father sat down. Muraco stared into the fire as Yuma noticed with horror that his father's shell began to change slowly into a murky gray color, all gloom and doom. It was as if Yuma was on the outside looking in. He reached out, but his hand merely passed through Muraco as if he was not there.

Muraco picked up a small bowl of water and drank; dark marks lined the bowl from where he put his lips. The old chief placed the bowl down on a rock near the fire. His end appeared to be near. Then Muraco began a death chant, and he soon disappeared into the dust. Yuma called out for his father, but the old chief was gone. There was only a slight wind. Then Yuma looked at the bowl of water near the fire; the marks were beginning to fade. He approached it and examined it closely. The fire was erasing the marks until the bowl became clear white.

Yuma turned and saw his own body still sitting a few yards away. He stumbled over to the body statue and fell forward into it.

*

The next morning, Yuma realized the power of his vision. He decided not to stay the extra day and instead left everything but his jug of water and began the long run back to the tribe. When he arrived, he told the elders of the village what he had experienced. They listened to the wild vision Yuma claimed he had, but the elders struggled to understand. Is fire erasing death marks? Over the next three days, they put all the pots and cups next to a raging fire, but people were still getting sick. Yuma argued that perhaps doing it once was not enough, but the elders refused to listen. They had judged his quest to be a fool's travel into the ether of the evil spirit. No one believed Yuma. Even Paco, his best friend, turned his back. Yuma was found unworthy to be chief of their tribe.

Chapter One
Appalachian Trail
1974
Looking for Adventure

It was a beautiful time of year, summer solstice, when the sun was at its peak and the temperature hovered around eighty degrees. But at night, the temperature would drop. In the mornings, when Tom started his hike, he wore a long-sleeved shirt, but after a few hours of hiking, he would be shedding garments down to the bare minimum.

Today, he was wearing his worn-out, sweat-stained T-shirt with a print of a psychedelic hand showing a peace sign and the words *Make Love Not War* printed across it. His long, brown hair was held back away from his youthful, oval-shaped face. He sported a burned-orange-colored bandana that went well with his chestnut-brown eyes. He had high, prominent cheekbones with flashing dimples that gave him a gentle, trustworthy look. But what stuck out the most were his angular, thick eyebrows that accented his eyes and gave him a deep, reflective, mysterious air. In addition, his physical prowess was well-suited for a young man looking for adventure.

Tom's favorite time of year was fall, still months away, when the foliage would be in full bloom with trees splashing red, gold, and purple. The forest, with its natural, abstract-scribbled lines and glorious colors, was a sharp contrast to the straight-line angles of buildings and the gray city skylines of Tom's hometown of Atlanta.

"Jesus." Tom eased his backpack down and put his hands on his knees, panting hard. His legs were trembling and crying out with pain. "I need to take a few minutes."

Tom nodded at Pat, a young man with the same spirit for hiking that he had met on the trail over a month ago. One of the nice outcomes of hiking the trail was meeting fellow hikers and, once in a while, partnering up with them.

"That last part of the trail was a bitch," Pat said as he inhaled deeply and exhaled sharply.

The trail was rocky with washed-out gullies and limbs that had fallen from previous storms. The hike was a harsh, steep incline that would burn a permanent memory in any good hiker.

"It reminded me of running stadium steps." Opening the side flap of his backpack, Tom pulled out a small book map. "Looks like the next shelter is about three miles farther."

"It's gonna be nice not to set up a tent."

"Yeah, all the comforts of a swanky hotel. Wouldn't you say, Mr. Patrick Kearney?" Tom replied as if he was talking to a hotel guest.

Both laughed, knowing that the shelter was nothing more than a big lean-to with wooden bunks. Some of the shelters had a fence covering the front with a gate. The fence was designed to keep bears and other animals out, which was great because you could keep your pack next to you instead of stringing it up on a limb twenty yards away. Hikers often learn that they need to do that when they wake up to a bear or raccoon tearing through their pack.

Pat took off his green shamrock baseball cap and scratched his head. He had flaming, shoulder-length red hair tied back in a ponytail with a bushy beard of the same color. His family descended from a long line of Irish and Scottish ancestry. "How about we meet at the shelter, laddie?" They agreed to split up and go their separate ways whenever they wanted some privacy or a different adventure or were just plain sick of each other. If one wanted to go off the trail and head into a town and the other wanted to stay on the trail, they would pull out their maps and pinpoint a spot and time to reunite. Pat continued, "If I detour off the trail, I'll leave my cap so you can see it; the bill will point in the direction I went."

Tom waved for Pat to get going as he started to stretch. "OK, see ya around the next bend."

A cramp was working its way up his thigh. The last thing Tom needed was to have a cramp in his legs. Sometimes in the middle of the night, after a particularly trying day on the trail, it felt like pliers were grabbing his thighs and twisting. Often, the pain drove him to cry.

It seemed to be easing now. *Thank God!* After Tom caught his breath, he opened a pack of freeze-dried tuna and Ritz crackers. For the trail, you had to pack light. He had freeze-dried salmon, chicken, some beef jerky, noodles, dehydrated fruit, granola bars, peanut butter tubes, and Snickers.

Time drifted away… But he had to catch up with Pat. Reluctantly, he went back to the trail and slipped on his pack. *OK, head 'em up, move 'em out.* Tom would go into a half-trance when he started hiking. It was a form of active meditation where he knew he was walking and climbing, but it felt like he was just floating along.

He was not very far away from the shelter, maybe a few more bends in the trail when he saw Pat's shamrock cap. The bill of the cap pointed to the left toward a smaller, less-taken, barely visible trail. This happened a lot on the AT, intersecting paths that forked off the main trail. Sometimes the only way you would know if you were on the right trail was to search for the trail paint marks, a simple slap of white paint across a tree. He took off his pack and slid it to the side of the trail under a shrub. He retrieved Pat's cap and went down the small path. About a quarter of a mile down the trail, Tom came to a small hillside. There were two men talking. He stepped off the path, leaned against a tree and listened, but he was too far away to make out what they were saying.

Tom knew it was never a good idea to suddenly appear at someone's campsite, so he edged his way around their blind side where he happened upon Pat. "Man, I am glad to see you." He handed over his friend's cap. "Have any idea what's going on over on that hilltop?" He pointed in the direction where he had seen the two men.

"I've been watching them. I think they are drug runners."

"What... why are they up here?"

"I overheard them talking about how their second stash house got raided in Waynesboro. A thru-town a few miles off the trail. It probably takes them a little while to get here, but I imagine it is a lot safer to hide your stash in the mountains than in town."

Tom thought he saw someone coming and ducked down quickly. Pat instinctively followed suit. They remained motionless and listened. There were always noises in the forest. Wind rattled trees and small animals scurried around, but nothing sounded quite like a human footstep, the clumsy thud unique to only that animal.

When they were sure there was no one around, they slowly lifted themselves. Finally, Tom spoke, "Sounds like they've taken a lesson from the ole whiskey runners. Cops don't tend to wander around the forest."

"Yeah, at any rate, their boss wanted to make sure they didn't get hit again, so they found this place. One of them said it was just temporary until things cool down."

"I don't think we want to mix it up with these guys." Tom nodded toward the trail. "Let's get the hell outta here."

"Where's your pack?" Pat asked.

"I took it off back at the trail, where you dropped your cap."

"OK, it's better if we split up, anyway. We'll make less noise. I'm going to circle over those hills." Pat pointed north. "I'll join you at the shelter."

Tom moved through the woods quietly but swiftly. Once he hit the trail, he looked for his pack. Nowhere. *I know it was there!* He checked again. Tom kneeled and angrily crawled around the bushes. He saw a shadow move over the ground. He looked up. He was staring down at the barrel of a Ruger Blackhawk .41 Magnum. Tom raised his hands slowly.

"Hey, I'm just a thru-hiker, mister."

"You lookin' for this pack, Bubba?" The guy asking was gangly with a high, pale forehead, stringy long hair, and a protruding tobacco-packed lip. "You with somebody?" He looked like he smelled something bad.

"No. I'm alone."

"If you are lying, I'll kill him and you."

"I tell ya, I'm alone."

"Name?"

"Tom Hunt." As soon as he said it, he wished he had used a fake name.

"OK. Call me Texas. Put your pack on; I'm marching your ass to our campsite." He had a pronounced hillbilly twang.

Texas, how phony can you get? Why did I give this bastard my real name?

Their walk was an awkward hike, with Tom having to hold his hands locked behind his head. Occasionally, they stopped, listening to anyone else around. This guy was visibly paranoid.

They arrived at a cleared-out space where there was a small campfire warming a beat-up coffee pot. "Drop the pack." As Tom obeyed, Texas pushed him roughly to the ground. Then, from straight out of the brush, a man approached and stood menacingly in front of Tom. He pulled out a pistol, the same kind of gun as his partner, and aimed it at Tom. He had a thick wrestler's body and looked very hard and mean. His head was shaven, and he had a thick black beard with matching eyebrows.

"Where did this fuckhead come from?" he asked in a thick accent that Tom thought reeked of Yankee New York Italian. He was holding the pistol in his left hand, with a chunky silver bracelet peering out beneath the cuff of his long-sleeved shirt.

"I found him coming down our path. He claims his name is Tom Hunt. I think he's been snooping his nosy ass around."

Texas kicked Tom and pointed him over to a tree. "Tie him up, Bama."

Tom laughed to himself. *Bama, you have got to be kidding me. The name Bama with a New York Yankee accent fits like a preacher in a strip club.* "Is everybody around here named for a southern state?" Tom asked.

Bama ambled over to Tom without responding, grabbed his right foot roughly, untied his boot string, and then unlaced it. He did the same to his left boot. After he unlaced the strings, he tied them together, grabbed Tom's hands, and twisted them behind his back. He tied him tightly to the nearest tree. The string was rough and hurt his wrist. It was irritating as hell. They would be blistered and raw, if not bleeding, in a few hours.

Bama walked nervously back and forth in front of Tom. "Stop clomping, Bama! For God's sake, I got to think. Now stay put," Texas snapped.

Tom's wrists and hands started to ache. *It will be dark soon. Pat had to be out there somewhere by now, just waiting for the right moment.*

Texas started walking away. "Let's wait for the boss. He said he would be here today. He'll decide what to do with this guy. For now, let's get back to work. We need to bag up some coke, MDA, and some brown sugar."

Wow, I wonder how much of that shit they have hidden up here.

If Tom was glued to the tree before, he was now frozen as he watched three more men walk into the campsite. Two of them looked as rough as the Italian wrestler, while the third one was clean-shaven and wearing spotless clothes and new boots. He tossed a dark blue denim backpack onto the ground.

Bama smiled. "Hello, capo Rogillio."

"Shut up, you idiot." The capo stepped over to Bama. "I said never to use our names when we are working." He slapped Bama across the cheek with a loud smack. "Now the kid knows my name." His eyes pinched together narrowly. "I also said, never use my title around people."

"I'm sorry, Kentucky." Bama rubbed the side of his face, looking like a punished dog. "Just so used to saying it; it just rolled off my tongue."

Great, another southern state for a name. Tom shook his head at their game.

"Who the hell is this guy?" Kentucky asked as he leaned down to examine Tom.

Texas explained, "He's been snooping around, boss."

"No, I wasn't. Just hiking the trail, man. I swear it."

"Shut up." Texas threatened with a cocked fist.

So, he's the leader of this outfit. Tom squinted his eyes and looked closely. *Square jaw, cleft chin, salt and pepper short hair, around 6' maybe 180 lbs. He was wearing a fringed buckskin jacket, aviator glasses, and a studded belt. A very hip look for stomping around the forest.*

Kentucky walked over to Tom. "What are you... twenty-something?"

Tom stared ahead and said nothing. Kentucky kicked Tom on the foot. "Answer me, or I'll beat the living shit out of you!"

Tom looked at him, his eyes full of hate. "Twenty-two."

"Twenty-two, full of piss and vinegar, and in deep trouble with the wrong guys! We're going to have to pack everything up. Let's move everything to our next backup stop."

"Boss, we've just gotten settled here. We can't scramble just because some guy happens to stroll in on us.

Besides, he's seen who we are," Bama complained. "We got to get rid of him."

"You knew this place was just temporary." The boss turned sharply and walked up into Bama's face again. "Look, if this jerk found us, others will, too. Besides, what do you suggest? Do you want to shoot him? Or what? Cut his throat? And then what, bury him?"

Bama scratched the back of his neck. "I could throw him off a cliff."

Out of the corner of his eye, Tom saw Pat lurking behind a log. He gave a deep sigh of relief. *The cavalry has arrived.*

"Fuck it! So far, we have no murders on our hands. We're gonna keep it that way. Pack up the goods and take them to our other drop spot," Kentucky said.

Texas showed the others where their present stash hole was. The drugs were nicely hidden in small canisters inside a small cave with an opening that could be easily covered. The area was extremely rocky, making it the perfect place.

"First, I have an order. Put these drugs," he handed Bama a piece of paper with a list on it, "in my backpack." He looked back at Tom, put his arm around the bald, bearded wrestler, and whispered, "Bama, after you guys get everything and are about to head out, I want you to shoot the boy up with the purest mad dog we got."

Bama smiled. "You want an OD?"

"No, I just said no murders; just give him enough that he will be loony tunes for a day while we get the hell out of here," Kentucky whispered through his coffee-stained teeth. "We'll never see him again." The boss patted Bama on the shoulder went over to a log and sat down, waiting for the others to finish carrying out his orders.

The men packed their stash and passed a couple of blunts of pot around. Before heading out, Texas decided to mess with Tom a little bit and kicked him savagely in the ribs. The others just laughed and kept smoking. Nightfall was approaching. The temperature was dropping fast. The only thing that helped Tom forget the cold was his bruised and battered ribs and his bleeding wrists.

The sun started to dip over the ridge when Kentucky told everybody but Bama to head out. When they got out of sight, Bama doused kerosene on a few big logs. He had arranged them for a fire. "Tom, you'll enjoy watching this fire after you zoom off to Wonderland." Tom watched as the man mixed some powders with water, no heat.

"I think you will enjoy this sixty mg of MDA." Bama had his syringe ready. Kneeling next to Tom, he pulled Tom's chin up and found a vein in his neck. Tom jerked slightly when felt the prick of the needle. "Now, now, this will only take a few seconds." He stood up from Tom. "I have always wanted to experiment with the jugular veins. If I miss and hit your carotid artery, well, the boss said he didn't want an OD, but if I did it wrong, you will be in for a slow and painful death." Bama smiled, very pleased with himself at the moment. "Dang, I guess accidents happen. Hell, as he said, we will never see your ass again anyway, so Kentucky will not know if I screwed up."

He was giving Tom enough for at least a five-hour trip, maybe more. If Tom survived, he would be waking up groggy and disoriented for another six or so hours. If he survived.

"I'm giving you a real treat. A mix of MDA with a perfect touch of LSD. We call it candy flip. Of course, the way we give candy flips is a little different. We give LSD first and then wait three hours before giving the MDA. But trust me, I am sure you will love it, anyway."

Tom jerked slightly when felt the prick of the needle. The injection stung like crazy. Tom could feel it burn and tingle as it traveled through his veins. Anything this painful had to be horrible for him. The onset took about twenty seconds, and the burning stopped at about the same time. He became very aware of his breathing. Soon, he felt a warm sensation all over his body, and the colors of the fire became much brighter.

"You look like you're just about over the rainbow," Bama said. "Have fun, son, and if I ever see you again… I'll kill your ass." He checked Tom's eyes. His big, dark-saucer eyes were a sure sign that he was going to be high for a long time. Then, with his big pocketknife, Bama cut Tom loose.

Tom felt the warm sensations running through his body getting stronger. The sunlight was almost gone, but everything appeared so vibrant. He held up his hand and slowly waved it in front of his face. A long trail of golden dust followed it. He pulled his other hand up, held them a few inches apart, and felt the heat. He looked at the ground; his head was just above the dust line of the earth. Slowly, he stood up and took a step forward. It was like stepping through fog or walking on air. He glanced around at the trees, which were breathing and making a rustling noise. He fell to his knees as he felt the magnetic pull of a black hole. As he was sucked down into the quicksand of swirling matter, he flipped and twisted, skydiving without a parachute.

Chapter Two
Atlanta, Georgia
1957
Magical Expressions

A psychedelic vision. Certainly not his first. But this intense? Never. *What the hell is happening to me?* he thought as he continued to flip madly as he fell down the black hole.

Tom passed through the black hole only to land in a huge cavern. There were magnificent multicolored stalagmites and stalactites. Most of them shined with an unusual buff yellowish-cream color, but some were brownish-red, and a few rare ones captivated Tom's attention as he walked past them. They were brilliant blue. There was a large iron portal in the distance. He walked cautiously toward it until he saw a huge carving of a Celtic knot. A brilliant spark of light streaked through the crack beneath the door. There was a large clock mounted at eye level with the hands stuck on 11:11 and the year 1957 written across it. Several pennies were spread out across the ground in front of the door. He picked up a handful of them. They all had the same mint year, 1898. That was the year his Nana was born, two years before the turn of the century. He stood staring at the pennies and thinking about his beloved grandmother. When he was a small boy, she taught him how to tell time and whistle. When he became a strong youth, he helped her every year in her football-field-sized organic garden. At harvest time, he helped cut, pick, and shuck the corn. There was nothing better than eating fresh corn, cucumbers, beans, tomatoes, and squash. But most importantly, she taught him to live life each day as if it were your last. She understood the philosophy of 'be here now' and lived it better than anyone Tom had ever met.

Tom put his hand on the door and felt the iron replicate of the Celtic knot. He knocked. No one answered. He waited and then pounded on the door with his fist. Still no answer. There was no other way to pass. Seemingly out of nowhere, a loud, rusty creaking noise reverberated as the door slowly opened. The sound of an ancient horn came from the other side. And there was light, so bright, so intense. "Hello, anyone there?" No one answered. Tom covered his eyes as he gently and slowly walked into the bright light. He heard the massive door close behind him. Tom shut his eyes tightly, avoiding the bright light, but still, he could see. The temperature had dropped to an uncomfortable yet not harsh cold. A long, spiraling path lay ahead, covered with lush green moss. Tom followed the path for miles and found himself in front of a two-story brick home. Wow! It was his childhood house. There, in the yard, he saw a boy playing. Tom realized he was looking at his childhood self.

He saw a scrappy young boy who was tall for his age and stronger than most. His brown hair was in a crew cut with the sides trimmed flat. The front of his hair was waxed up and short. He had big brown eyes and a devilish little smile, complete with dimples. One of his front teeth had already fallen out or had been knocked out from his constant roughhousing.

The year 1957 was a busy year for the world. Egypt had nationalized the Suez Canal and run the British and French out. Israel began military operations against Egypt, the Asian flu pandemic killed over a million people worldwide, Russia launched their first artificial satellite, Sputnik 1, and started the space race, and federal troops were used to ensure that nine African Americans could attend a high school in Little Rock, Arkansas, the French left Vietnam while the US Military Assistance Advisory Group assumed full responsibility for training South Vietnamese forces. The first Frisbee toy was cleverly mass-marketed. It sold tens of millions.

On the economic front, a gallon of gas was twenty-four cents, the average cost of a new house was around twelve thousand dollars, the average wages per year were a little over four thousand dollars, and the minimum hourly rate was one dollar.

Today, a semi-cold, cloudless day in February, was Thomas William Hunt's birthday. Tom was out in the backyard playing with his closest friend. They were sword-fighting with sticks and chasing each other around the large oak tree in the middle of the yard. Occasionally, they dropped their swords and would fight in hand-to-hand combat, throwing each other to the ground and wrestling until they were too tired to continue.

Young Tom was so engaged that he didn't hear his father driving up to the house and climbing the twenty-two steps from the turnaround to the backyard. His father, Dr. Stephen Hunt, had been a cardiologist at Greystone University Hospital for the past decade. He stopped at the top of the stairs and watched Tom run to pick up a stick and begin thrashing it into the air, shouting at his friend to surrender. "Tom!" His father put down his briefcase and yelled louder, "Hey, Tom!"

Stopping in his tracks, Tom looked over at his dad. He immediately dropped his pretend sword and ran over for a big hug. His father was a tall man with a kind, round face, and short, black, wavy hair. His dark horn-rimmed glasses projected an air of intelligence, and the white, heavily starched medical doctor's coat that he always wore signaled his importance in the world.

"What are you up to, Tom?" his father asked.

"Sword fighting," Tom said, still winded.

"I see."

Tom's mother, Natalie, came out of the house wearing a nice dark blue-and-white polka dot dress and black heel pumps to greet her husband. She gave him a quick kiss on the cheek, leaving behind a mark of her playfully feminine red lipstick. She was always well-manicured, and her hair was artistically kept in the popular 50s bouffant hairstyle. When she added jewelry, she looked radiant.

"You look tired, Steve. But I have some good news; Savannah cooked up some of her fried chicken for tonight's dinner."

Savannah was their black housekeeper and cook. She came five days a week and was like a second mother to Tom. She told him what to do and, in the absence of his mother, even punished him if he acted up, which was often. "I see Tom is playing with his friend again." Steve pointed to an empty yard.

"He has been all afternoon. Did you talk to the psychiatrist?"

"Yes," he rubbed Tom's head, "son, go clean-up for your birthday dinner."

He waited until Tom let the back screen door slam and was out of sight. "I had a lunch meeting with him. Unless Tom is using his imaginary companion as a way of blaming bad behavior, he wouldn't worry about it. Tom will grow out of it."

"Honey, I think it's strange. Tom is playing and talking to an invisible boy all the time." Natalie's eyes flared with frustration and some embarrassment. "I asked my friends in the bridge club, and not one of them said their child had an imaginary friend. Not one."

"It's going to be okay, honey, I promise."

"He even wanted me to set an extra plate at dinner for his friend." She sighed heavily. "For God's sake, when is this going to stop?"

"As I said, it will be okay." Steve picked up his briefcase.

"The psychiatrist did ask if Tom had a pet."

"What kind of pet?"

"Any kind." Steve shrugged. "Something he is responsible for."

"OK, then." Natalie paused for a moment, and then stated with one eyebrow cocked, "I will get him a small pet turtle tomorrow, and he will have to feed it and change the water."

"Good plan."

"I'll get the turtle, but I put my foot down on him, pretending there is somebody eating dinner with us that doesn't exist."

They strolled to the house. After the doctor sat down, she brought him a glass of chardonnay. "So, did anything happen today at work?"

"Yes, I have to fly to DC tomorrow. Senator Mason is not feeling well."

Tom's father was finishing up his military commitment back in 1952 at Bethesda Hospital when Mason, the majority leader of the Senate, had a heart attack. Steve saved his life and became his cardiologist. Everything changed in the Hunt family after that event. As a result of being the primary physician to a powerful United States Senator, Steve was sent on special assignments. Kings, presidents, and dictators around the world became his patients. He even watched over Martin Luther King Jr.'s father, Papa King.

*

The next day, Tom and his mother went to a pet store and bought a little green turtle. Tom was thrilled to have it and he named him Peek-A-Boo because the turtle kept hiding his head. Tom took responsibility for feeding and changing the water every day. He played with it outside. But one day when he went to feed his turtle, he didn't hide his head. The turtle didn't swim. He didn't even move. Tom ran to get his mother. When she looked into the small aquarium, there was no doubt the turtle was dead.

Natalie never beat around the bush. She told you the reality of a situation and then she expected you to get over it and move on with life. "Tom," she cupped his little head in her hands and said, "your turtle has died."

Tom blinked his big brown eyes. "He died?"

"Yes, he has gone to heaven." She patted him on the head and made her way to the laundry room and came back with a small box. She placed the turtle into the box and handed it to Tom. "I want you to go in the backwoods and find a nice place to dig a hole with your army shovel and then place this box into the hole and cover him up."

"Why?"

"Because when a turtle or any animal dies, that is what we do. We bury them."

"Oh." Tom's eyes began to swell with tears. "Does that mean I won't see him anymore?"

"I'm afraid not, Tom, but he will always be a part of you."

Tom followed his mother's orders and marched into the backwoods. He dug a hole deep enough to bury two of the little boxes. He covered the box with dirt and then felt a strange presence. He looked around but saw nothing. Nothing, until he looked up into the trees. Three-fourths of the way up, a tall oak tree was a sight that made him stumble backward.

A man with a long, flowing, angelic white beard and matching hair was in the tree, or rather, was hovering next to it. His arms were sculptured muscle. But the most salient physical attribute was the large, glowing white wings that were attached to his back and extended down beyond his feet. Waves of energy pulsated with radiant colors so powerful Tom had trouble keeping his eyes on him. He felt his heart pounding as he turned and ran back to his house, screaming for his mother. He found her in the kitchen making lunch.

"Mom... Mom." He could hardly breathe. "I saw something out there. It was up high in the trees and had big wings and light and..."

His mother turned and interrupted, "Calm down, son. You probably saw a reflection or something."

"No Mom, I buried the turtle as you said, and then this big light was up in the tree. I tell you, there was something there."

"Of course, I believe you, dear." She had just finished making Tom's sandwich. "Here dear, I made you a nice peanut butter and jelly sandwich." She poured him a glass of milk. "We'll talk about it when your dad comes home."

After hearing the story, Tom's father called the psychiatrist for advice. As a result of their conversation, their family preacher was invited to come by the house on Saturday. It was decided that Tom's turtle should have a proper "goodbye." So, Tom, his father and mother, and the preacher walked to the turtle's grave, huddled around together, and held hands as the preacher shared a few words of the gospel.

Chapter Three
Appalachian Trail
1974
Mind's Eye

Tom was breathing. At least he was aware of that. The air slowly made its way into his lungs, and then his chest dropped, and the air rushed out. There was a sound. A sound far away in the distance, but it was now getting closer and louder.

"Tom! Wake up, Tom!" Pat screamed as he checked his friend's pulse. "Come on, man, wake up!" Tom moaned and gave several strong grunts. His eyes opened. "That's it, Tom, come on around, man." Pat started patting Tom on the jaw.

Tom turned on his side and began spewing puke. "My stomach is killing me! It just came out of nowhere!" Tom continued puking dark-brown drool and bits of food. It smelled of rotten eggs and spoiled fish. Tom gasped for air but felt another surge of burning puke. Vomit covered Tom's shirt.

Pat was holding him. "Don't worry Tom, I'm here with you." Tom nodded his appreciation. He had another surge in his gut, but this time, he only dry heaved. Pat continued, "I don't know what that guy gave you, but ever since they left, I have been taking care of you. For God's sake, I thought you were going to OD." They huddled together as Tom slowly regained his senses.

"Wow, that was scary, Tom."

Tom nodded as he whispered, "That was a hell of a trip." He turned around and with help from Pat, he sat up. His face was caked with dirt from crawling and rolling on the ground. Tom was still groggy and felt the beginning sting of a terrible drug hangover.

"Let's make camp here and let that shit get out of your system." Pat handed Tom a small canteen of water.

Tom took a long swig and then asked, "What about the assholes? They could come back."

"Not a chance, Tom. They're long gone."

After Pat set up camp, Tom changed his shirt and crawled into his sleeping bag. He passed out and slept for the next twelve hours. Too tired to dream. Too tired to eat anything.

*

The next morning, Tom felt like a truck had run over him, but he was determined to get the hell out of there. He fumbled around in his pack until he found some extra shoestrings. It would have been tough trying to tramp through the woods without them.

After a small breakfast of a single granola bar, they began to hike. It was a slow hike. Very slow. Time was not important. How far they hiked was not important. But for

Tom, returning to the trail was important. Nothing was going to stop him, not even near death.

It was a tough hike. Tom's legs were still shaky, and he had to stop often to get his breath. They kept hiking until Tom slipped badly on some slippery rocks and went down hard. Pat was fast to try and help Tom up, but Tom waved him off. "No, I'm okay," he said as he pushed himself to get up and continue.

"When we get to the top of this ridge, Tom, I think we should stop for the day," Pat suggested.

"How far do you think we've hiked?" Tom asked.

"I would say, four, maybe five miles."

Tom shook his head. "I'm not ready to stop."

"Don't be foolish, Tom. Let's set up—"

"I said no!" Tom interrupted, "if you want to stop, then stop. But I am going to push on for a few miles more."

"Why Tom? What are you trying to prove? Or what the hell are you testing?"

Tom laughed. "I don't know for sure; I just know that I got to keep pushing." They kept moving, but at a slower speed.

"OK, but I would like to know why?"

"You want to know why I have to push so hard right now?"

"Yes, why? We have stopped along the trail many times before to get some rest."

"It's one thing to test yourself when everything is perfect. The weather is nice, you feel great, and you're emotionally ready. But that's when it's easy. The real test is when everything is screwed up."

"And now you know?" Pat asked.

"This isn't the absolute bottom of the barrel worst it could be, but now is the time to push it."

"OK, I can buy that."

Tom nodded and picked up his speed. Hours later, they found a place to camp.

It felt really good when Tom pulled off his boots. He sat right on them in a half-lotus position. "I still don't feel hundred percent; I wonder if I ever will?"

Pat sat on a small log and pulled a container out of his backpack. It kept his weed and papers dry. Tom watched in admiration as Pat rolled a joint with one hand. He lit it up, inhaled deeply, and handed it to Tom. "Here, this will take the edge off," he said, choking back the smoke.

Tom took a deep draw and felt much, much better; the nausea he had felt all day disappeared, and he was relaxed, euphoric even. "Acapulco Gold?"

"Yep, this is the last of it."

"How about the Panama Red?"

"Finito, miles ago."

Tom frowned. "We could probably hunt something down in the next town that's not too far off the trail."

Pat told Tom to take it easy while he collected wood. He placed a bundle of twigs, sticks, and small logs next to Tom. Leaning forward, Tom laid out a small fire and lit it. The glowing yellow and orange colors of the flickering flames began to mesmerize him.

Tom rubbed his eyes; they were heavy, dry, and tired. He was glad he didn't have a mirror; he was afraid of not recognizing himself. He started his hike as a polished college kid with clean clothes. He was well groomed, complete with Old Spice cologne splashed all over his body. Now, even God wouldn't recognize him. His beard was scraggly, and his long hair was entangled. He needed shampoo and a serious trim. His fingernails were filthy, packed black with dirt.

"Been thinking about my drug experience. The vision. It was so real." Tom stared at the fire.

"What did you see, Tom?" Pat picked up a stick and poked the fire. "If you like, I'll give you my take on it."

Tom nodded. "I came to this huge iron portal. On the ground, pennies were lying around, and there was a clock stuck on the time, 11:11."

"That's pretty cosmic, Tom!" Pat jabbed at the fire. A small flame shot up.

"You sound like you know a lot about this spiritual stuff."

"Some." Pat's eyes sparkled. "My grandmother taught me."

"Your grandmother?"

"You won't understand this, but she was a…"

"A what? Go on, Pat. Spit it out."

"She was a Celtic witch."

"What?" Tom's face twisted in disbelief. "That's crazy."

"Yeah, well, I saw her demonstrate many of her powers with my own eyes, Tom. She could interpret people's dreams and visions. She cast powerful spells. People came from all around to get her help."

"And she taught you how to do it?"

"She taught me a little bit about it, and she taught me about the stars," Pat said.

"Well," Tom shrugged his shoulders, "I don't have a clue on how to interpret this vision, so have at it."

Pat reached over and patted his shoulder. "Go on, tell me what you remember."

"The pennies had the year my grandmother was born on them."

"She was letting you know she would protect you on your journey. That she was with you."

"And the clock?"

"It is telling you that you are spiritually stuck. Time is not linear in the spiritual world." Pat poked the fire again and a small flame flashed upward. "Your spirit is trying to tell you that you need to live your own life, not what others plan for you or how they expect you to live."

"That certainly fits. I was brought up from day one with a pile of expectations."

"What was the weirdest part of your vision?"

"Weirdest?"

"Yes, something that really stunned you."

Tom sighed. "I guess the weirdest experience was that I could see with my eyes closed."

"The reason you could see with your eyes closed was that the drugs tapped into your third eye. It was difficult to tap into, given the size of the iron portal. But it finally cracked it open."

"I have heard about this third eye; what is it?"

Pat put another log on the fire. "It is said that the third eye is the dormant pineal gland. It resides between the two hemispheres of your brain. The third eye can detect things subconsciously as small as an atom, and it is the gateway to your spiritual experiences."

"I know it is written about in a lot of religions."

"Yes. Buddhism, Taoism, Hinduism, and even the Bible mentions it."

"So, do you study all those religions?" Tom asked.

"I study anything that helps me understand more about the cosmic world."

"I would like to know more about it."

"I am sure you will learn."

For some time, they pondered the fire, discussing the mysteries of the universe, and then rolled out their sleeping bags. They were on their backs looking at the stars. Pat pointed. "Over there is Sagittarius."

"All I see is a bunch of random stars."

"The archer represents a centaur half man, half horse, and he carries a bow and arrow. He was a great hunter."

"Nope, don't see it," Tom replied.

"OK, how about I give you an easy one?" Pat pointed to a different spot. "Look over there and you will see Cygnus. What does that constellation look like to you?"

"A big X."

"Come on Tom, use your imagination. Cygnus is a swan swimming up the stream of the Milky Way."

"Yeah, my knowledge of the stars stops with horoscopes." Tom yawned.

"By the time you finish the trail with me, you'll know a lot more." Pat added, "You need to know the myth behind these constellations. Each story tells us something about human nature. Some stories portray the evil side of nature: murder, betrayal, greed, passion, vanity, jealousy, and power. Some portray the good side of nature: love, compassion, generosity, trust, and friendship. You see, Cygnus was a beautiful story of friendship."

"That's good." Tom rolled onto his side, facing away from Pat.

"Two young gods were racing across the skies when they fell to earth. One sank to the bottom of a river. His friend was so distraught that he begged Zeus to turn him into a swan so he could dive to the bottom and save his friend. He was successful, and Zeus was so moved he immortalized this act of bravery by putting the swan in the stars."

Pat waited to hear Tom's response to the beautiful story. All he heard was the steady breathing of sleep.

*

Tom woke up cold, tired, and hungry. They rarely talked to each other first thing in the morning, but Pat broke their unwritten rule of silence. "You said that you came to the mountains to learn more about yourself. To test yourself. So, besides what you just went through, what has been your toughest trial?"

Tom picked up a small pot of hot water, poured it into a cup, and started bouncing a tea bag around. He blew into the cup to cool it enough to have a sip. *Sweet Jesus, that tastes good.*

"I think… my emotional state. The first thing I noticed was the heartstrings of love yanking at me and yanking hard. My college girlfriend, Callie, didn't understand why I was so hell-bent on hiking around the country. I had graduated from college, and I knew she was expecting an engagement ring; not someone who was going to run away to the mountains for God knows how long and for what kind of adventures."

"So, how are you feeling right now?"

Tom sighed. "I am still sorting that out, but I know deep down inside, my gut is telling me I have to finish what I started."

Pat gently nodded his agreement. Tom thought about Callie; he could see her smiling. *No, don't think about her, stop it!* He shook his head, trying to knock her out of his head. Tom didn't want to talk about Callie.

"How long have we been together on the trail?" Tom asked.

"We met a couple of months ago after your fraternity brothers bailed. I don't know how long you were on it before we got together." Pat shrugged. "Hell, the way we look and smell now, I would guess many months."

Tom smelled his shirt. "When I go off the trail next time, I'm not riding in the back of a trash truck."

"Hey, that may be all that will pick you up."

Tom checked his backpack. He was down to his last freeze-dried pack of tuna. "Speaking of town, I've got to hit the next town. We need supplies." He had already lost fifteen pounds, and he didn't have any more fat to lose. Only muscle would be lost now. "How come you never come to town with me?"

"It's simple; I don't like people." Pat had water boiling in a small camper pot. It was best to never drink the water without boiling it first. Playing Russian roulette with bacteria or parasites was not an experienced hiker's idea of a good time. Pat poured the water into a canteen and took a long swing of water. Tom admired his friend's physical powers. His red hair and beard made him into a Celtic warrior of sorts. He was a mountain of a man, all muscle. *Why wasn't he losing weight?*

"You don't have to like people to go to town with me. Don't you ever want to sit back with a cold beer and just look around a little?"

"Every time you come back from town, you have a story, and they are never good ones. You remember the first story you came back with… The time you went into a place called The Exit Inn Bar."

Tom rolled his eyes. "Come on, man, nothing happened to me; it was just a weird place."

"Let's see. You told me you went in and ordered a beer. You were watching the locals shoot pool. Some local bands were playing awful country music. The place was packed with Saturday night couples dancing away. Have I got the setting about right so far?"

"Yes, so far."

"Then you saw a small woman come into the bar and walk briskly, with laser-like intent, to the center of the dance floor. Then she cold-cocked a lady clean out of nowhere."

Tom nodded. "Yep, then she started choking her and screaming obscenities."

"And you say nobody even attempted to break up the fight, but instead, they cheered it on. That's certainly human nature."

"Well, they pulled her off eventually," Tom added.

"And this is the sort of adventure you want me to share with you?"

"It's not always like that, Pat. You always focus on the brutal negatives. There is a lot of good out there, too."

"Yeah, there is a lot of good, Tom." Pat shook his head. "But when you deliberately go into places that harbor violence, greed, and emptiness, you will find yourself attracting more of the same. It gathers on your soul like lint on clothes. You need to remember that what you do is what happens to you. It's the law of attraction. Right now, I just want to work on myself. So, if you don't mind, I will pass on the town trips you like so much."

Tom laughed.

"What? What's so funny?"

"After college, when I told my father I was going to hike the AT, his jaw dropped to the floor. He thought for sure I was going to tell him I wanted to go to grad school and marry Callie. He asked me why. Why do you want to hike the Appalachian Trail? He was totally befuddled."

Pat cocked his head back and looked down his nose at Tom. "So, what was your answer?"

"I told him I wanted to find myself."

"And he said?"

"He came over to me and put his arms around me and asked: 'Son, how does one lose themselves?'" Tom swallowed hard and shrugged his shoulders. "I didn't know what to say; I just shook it off."

Pat lowered his head in reflection on what Tom's father had said. He looked up at Tom and mused, "Your dad was right; you can never actually lose yourself, but you can ignore looking deeper into yourself. This is your opportunity to do that, Tom. Look deep."

Chapter Four
Appalachian Trail
1974
Earlier On the Trail

There was constant light rain. *Thank God for my poncho.* The trail was muddy and slick. Tom's boots stuck into the ground with every step. Presently, around a long bend, he saw something move.

"Pat."

"Yeah, I see it."

"What is it?"

"I think it's a red fox." They watched as the fox circled round and round.

"It looks disoriented," Pat said.

"Looks like it's having some kind of seizure. *Hmmm…*"

"Yeah, what the hell is wrong with it?"

"My guess is it has rabies," Tom said. The fox stopped, lowered its head to the ground, and stared at them, growling.

"Best get our walking sticks ready, Tom. He's going to charge us."

As soon as Pat gave the warning, the fox charged. It dodged Pat's swing and snapped at his leg, ripping his pants. Tom swung down as hard as he could, hitting the fox on the head. Crack! The fox stumbled and fell.

"Put it out of its misery, Tom."

Tom jabbed his walking stick into the fox's throat and pressed down hard. Blood oozed down, making a small dark-red puddle in the dirt. "Did he bite you? Scratch you?"

Pat pulled up his torn pants. Tom took a good look at his leg. "No damage to the skin." Tom shook his head. "Whew, that was a close one."

Pat pointed to the fox. "I think we should bury it, so no animals eat it. Do you know, can they get rabies from that?"

"I'm not sure."

"To be on the safe side, let's bury it."

Tom thought about how he would have responded to the fox when he first started out on the trail in Georgia. Back then, he and his buddies would have been running in the opposite direction in fear. Tom burst out laughing, thinking about how he first started his journey.

*

The Past: College Buddies

In the beginning, he had three fraternity brothers tagging along. They had nice, shiny, new equipment; Jansport backpacks, top-of-the-line sleeping bags, dome-shaped tents, and Timberland water-resistant boots. They looked like clean-cut young men fresh from country clubs. They screamed of money and, as Charles Dickens would say they, "shine like cherub's cheeks."

They were naïve, with idealist views of what hiking in the forest primeval would bring their way. They expected Walden Pond and the beauty of nature. But there is always the other side of the coin. The pain, the danger, the bugs. The balance of life.

It didn't take long for their clothes to be saturated with smoke and sweat from long, tedious hikes. Mud was caked on their boots from the heavy rains, and dirt marred their coats. Their beards looked patchy and sparse, and their hair shabby and uncombed. Looking like that, they wouldn't even be allowed to pick up the trash at a country club.

Tom's fraternity brothers had thought it was going to be nothing but fun. Their mindset was wrong from the beginning, and Tom figured they would bail as soon as reality hit them in the face.

With their upbringing. There was never a doubt that they would go to college, and never a doubt that they would go on to an advanced degree. Oh, you had a choice; you could become a physician, get your Ph.D., become a lawyer, or an executive in business. Your choice, though. But nothing less. No pressure.

Alfred gave it up after just two weeks. He was a frail musician, a poet at heart. His major in college had been German. Alfred confided in Tom during their second year of college late one night after a fraternity party. He was a frustrated gay man and couldn't take it anymore. It was time for him to come out of the closet and he wanted Tom to be the first to know.

The fact that Alfred had told Tom showed a lot of courage and trust. Tom was not going to let him down. Their friendship was sealed.

Alfred was miserable on the trail from day one and made everyone else just as miserable. Tom got tired of his constant whining. Alfred had a list of things to bitch about; his pack was too heavy, the food sucked, the fire smoked too much, there was no music, and he always had a terrible night's sleep. But what sent Alfred packing was a harsh storm with violent winds. Walls of rain battered the ground and lightning flashed in the dark night. Alfred had been shaking in fear. It was a long night without sleep.

After the storm, Tom found Alfred sitting with his arms tightly crossed and a pissy face. It was time for Alfred to leave. He should never have come along in the first place. "Why are you out here, Alfred? This isn't your thing, man." Tom asked.

Alfred looked exhausted. "I just didn't know what to do after graduation, so I decided to stick around with you guys."

"It's not worth it if you are going to be miserable. Besides, you need to go to graduate school. That's where you belong."

Alfred nodded.

"I want you to do something for me." Alfred rubbed his eyes, exhaustion written across his pale face.

"I wish you would watch over Callie."

"You want me to check in with your college girlfriend while you're gone?"

"Yes, she likes you. You can help her understand why I have to do this." Tom put his hand on his friend's shoulder. "Can you help me out?"

"Tom, are you really just wanting me to spy on her?"

"No, I would never ask that. I need your help, Alfred. You're the only person I would trust to do this for me. I need you to make sure she knows I am thinking about her and that I love her. Just give her that message for me."

"OK. For you, Tom." Alfred didn't waste any time; he packed up immediately and headed back down the mountains.

It was only a few weeks later when the others bailed. Hunger drove them to go home and eat and get on with their lives. They had their little vacation after graduation. Tom wished them well.

Within a month, though, Tom missed his traveling buddies. He had thoughts about leaving the trail like his fraternity brothers. But he fought that impulse. *No way. I am not giving in.* He chanted that mantra over and over.

*

The Past: First Time Tom met Pat

It was late afternoon on a mild but windy day. Tom was following a stream, looking for a dry place to camp. That's when Tom saw a young man bathing in the stream.

"Hey buddy, that looks pretty damn refreshing!"

"It is."

The man stood up from the knee-high stream. He had long red hair and a matching beard. He was a man to admire. An athletic-looking guy with thick muscled legs and arms, and a chest to match. He smiled and waved to Tom. Wandering back over to the edge of the stream, he picked up a towel and started drying himself off. "Are you a thru-hiker?" His voice was deep and full of youthful confidence.

"I am, and you?" A jagged scar ran down from the corner of the man's left eye and disappeared into his beard. On his right shoulder was a large green tattoo of a Celtic knot.

"Yep, I'm heading north."

"Same," Tom replied.

"I have a campsite just around the bend if you want some company." Tom nodded.

They came to a small flat area surrounded by young trees. The man turned and stuck out his hand. "My name is Patrick Sean Kearney… Call me Pat."

"Mine's Tom Hunt." Tom returned a hearty handshake. "I must say, you have a strong Irish name."

"Patrick means noble, while Sean stands for God's grace, and Kearney translates to warrior."

"A noble warrior that stands with God's grace. Like I said, a strong Irish name." Tom pointed to his shoulder. "I like the tattoo as well. What is it?"

A big, wide smile eased across his face. "I had that done years ago. The Celtic knot has no beginning or end.

It represents the enduring nature of our spirit. Besides, my grandmother had one just like it."

Tom watched as Pat finally put on some underwear and blue jeans. He stopped short of putting on a shirt or shoes. He walked over to a fallen tree, looked at the dead branches, and then at Tom. "This old white ash is mostly dead and is perfect for a fire; besides ash doesn't spark or smoke much."

Tom watched as Pat snapped off some big limbs. Unlike Pat, Tom didn't have bulging barbell muscles, but instead a lean, wiry frame and a rock-hard belly. He was a good thirty pounds less than Pat and his build was much more suited for hiking.

They sat in silence, feeding wood to the fire. Once they got hungry, they invaded their packs. Pat's fare was similar to Tom's, except Pat had a dozen cans of Vienna sausage. Pat slapped a little sausage on a saltine cracker and shoved it in his mouth.

"Where's your tent?" Tom asked as he looked around the site.

"I don't put it up unless it looks like bad weather."

Tom looked up into the sky. "Sometimes the weather looks good when you crawl into your sleeping bag, but then it rains like crazy in the middle of the night. What do you do then?"

"You mean, besides getting my ass wet?"

Tom laughed. "Yes."

"I get up and put up my tent. But nine times out of ten, I can predict the weather pretty well."

"So, you are sleeping under the stars tonight?"
"Yep, and you?"
Tom nodded. "Yeah, I think I will."

*

The Past: First Night with Pat
Something woke Tom in the middle of the night. He sat up and listened. Luckily, the fire embers were still glowing. He picked up a small log and tossed it onto the fire. There was something moving across the ground. It slithered next to Tom. *Jesus.* He tried to back away, but froze. He tried to speak, but nothing came out. *Shit.* His eyes widened as the snake slithered next to his sleeping bag. Tom was stuck in his bag with nowhere to go.

Pat was awake now, lying on top of his sleeping bag. He rolled over and grabbed the snake behind its head, holding it carefully away from his body, about shoulder high as he stood up. The snake flailed around, slapping Pat's arm. "Well, look here, we got us a four-foot black rat snake." He brought it closer.

"That's okay; I don't need to see it."

Pat laughed. "He is one of the good guys out here, Tom."

"Maybe, but I can like him from afar."

"You ever eaten snake?"

"No."

"Wanna to try some?"

"No way."

"All right then." Pat sighed and threw the snake as far as he could. "That happens once in a while; they like the warmth of the fire."

"How... how did you know it wasn't poisonous?"

"I didn't. I didn't know what kind it was until I caught him."

Pat stretched his back and then laid back into his sleeping bag. Soon he was snoring.

You have got to be kidding. Who goes back to sleep after tangling with a snake? No way. Tom put more wood on the fire and kept his eyes wide open.

Early the next morning, Pat rolled over and looked at Tom. "Did you have a good night's sleep, after all?"

"I nodded off now and then. I couldn't get the snake out of my mind."

"Are you afraid of them?"

"Good guess."

"Well, the trail is made for you to face your fears."

Tom scrambled to his feet. "So, what are your fears, Pat?"

Pat stood up without using his hands. "Evil."

"Evil?"

"Yes, evil. The world is stalked by relentless evil."

"Well, I think snakes are evil."

Pat bent down and started rolling up his sleeping bag. "Tom, I am talking about supernatural evil." Tom was speechless; that sounded like a bunch of mind-fuckery to him.

On the one hand, he could learn a lot by partnering with Pat for a while. On the other hand, he was a bit strange. It was now or never. "Listen, Pat, I think I could learn a lot from you. Are you up for hiking together?

Pat laughed. "I never doubted it, Tom. I figured we met for a reason."

*

The Past: High School Sweetheart
Tom noticed a few quirks about Pat. He always wanted to be the lead hiker. He decided where they would camp, and if he didn't want to talk about something, he would grunt and walk off. Pat rarely talked when they were hiking. Tom liked that about Pat as it gave him a chance to let his mind drift. Tom often pictured, frequently from a third-person point of view, his past.

As Tom hiked, he felt his breathing, slow and deep. Slow and deep. His eyes cast down, he stepped over limbs, sidestepped branches, and could sense where the potholes were.

The rhythm of hiking took over and left him free to daydream. Tom let whatever came to his mind flow freely, unobstructed. Hours of daydreaming. Reliving the fun things he had done in the past. Reliving the things, he wished he hadn't done.

Tom fanned through a kaleidoscope of life events but settled on his high school girlfriend, Vicki. She had long, straight blonde hair that flowed to her mid-back. Her blue eyes shone, dominating her pleasantly round face. Tom had read in a magazine about how the Chinese believe your facial features portray your personality. Tom concluded that Vicki was sensual, lively, and wanted to live life to the utmost. He thought that was the perfect description of her.

Tom imagined himself knocking on the door of Vicki's house and having his customary chitchat with her parents. He took her to see a movie. Some stupid comedy. They sat in the back row. Vicki had snuck in a flask full of her parents' liquor in her handbag. This time, it was rum. She poured it into the Cokes that Tom had bought. There was enough to make them woozy.

After the movie, the real fun started. They went "parking" at Tom's church. He would leave the window open to his Sunday school. The room had nice big couches, unlike the small back seat of his father's car. Tom checked all three windows one by one. On that night, they seemed to be locked. He checked the windows for other rooms. Aha! One wasn't fully locked! It was the one next to the door to the sanctuary. Tom pushed a little harder, and the window gave way. He stretched his arm painfully, but finally opened the door.

He called Vicki. She didn't hesitate and went right into the church with him. So many rows of pews. The moonlight shone brilliantly through the massive stained-glass windows. Shadows loomed. A huge wooden cross was suspended in the air in front of the altar. The sheer silence was unnerving, and his adrenaline pumped. Tom hungrily unbuttoned her blouse, hugged her tightly, and eased them gently down onto the carpet. In the back of his mind, he had the nagging thought that Jesus was watching them from the huge cross in the front of the sanctuary, but Tom's fervent sexual appetite ruled the night.

Chapter Five
Waynesboro, Virginia
1974
Eye for an Eye
The Present

Rain was dripping from the brim of Tom's hat and his poncho was saturated. He was climbing a steep, slippery part of the trail, leaning on his walking stick. The stick was a gift from Pat. It was thick and sturdy and Pat had carved the small head of a man with a long, flowing beard on the handle. Tom enjoyed watching Pat whittle on it night after night, not knowing it was going to be his.

"Tom, let's break for a minute. I need to check the map." Tom nodded.

"So, you're dead set on going into town?" Pat asked.

"What's that?"

"I said, are you going into town?"

"Yes. It's only a few miles off the trail. It'll be an easy hitch to town from Rockfish Gap."

Tom liked the small towns in Virginia. The last Virginia trail town he stayed in was Damascus, and that was many miles of rough trail ago. Now he was about to head into Waynesboro.

"OK then, I think the trail you want is coming up soon."

Pat dug out his map. He pointed to a trail about a mile down. Then he traced with his finger where he was heading. "I'm heading up to McCormick Gap Overlook for tonight," Pat said as he traced his fingernail across the map, "and then I'll head over to Calf Mountain Shelter and wait for you there. It looks like Calf Mountain Shelter is only about ten miles from here. So, I'll get plenty of rest."

"Perfect. I'll meet ya in two to three days."

The rain was slowing down and turned into a heavy mist by the time they got to their separation point on the trail. Pat waved, nodded goodbye, and kept hiking.

"Later, Pat," Tom said as he detoured off the main trail.

He hiked to a small mountain road. He was excited to be hitchhiking. Two cars whizzed by, spraying him down good. One guy slowed down, but took a closer look and sped off. A long time passed before a blue Mustang pulled over. The driver was a young woman. She had brunette hair with innocent-looking hazel eyes. Even sitting down, Tom could see that she was taller than average.

"Wow! Looks like you've been on the trail for a long time." Her smile made Tom smile.

"Yes, it's been a while."

Tom tossed his backpack in the back seat and got in. She stuck out her hand. "I'm Amber Jackson."

As they shook hands, Tom felt the tightness of her grip. It was firm. *She's probably a strong-minded woman.*

"Hello Amber, I'm Tom Hunt."

"Nice to meet you, Tom." Amber eased slowly back onto the road.

"Nice wheels."

"Thanks, Tom, it's my dream car."

"I've always heard that the car you own tells a lot about you."

"Oh, what does my Mustang say about me?"

"A car like this tells me you like a little danger in your life."

Amber nodded. "What else?"

"A sports car as fine as this tells me you probably get a lot of attention."

"*Hmm*, I have to think about that one."

"There is one more."

"What?"

"You prefer cool over comfort. I have never found a Mustang that sits comfortably, and they always rattle." Tom wiggled in his seat.

She laughed. "There is some truth to that one."

Amber kept her eyes on the curvy mountain road. She was at ease driving in the mountains. She was going well over the speed limit. She barely slowed down on the hairpin turns.

"You live around here?" Tom asked.

"Yes, for now; I own a condo in Waynesboro."

"What do you mean for now?"

"I'm behind on my payments. I'm a bartender, and every month, it's a struggle to pay all my bills."

"I... I'm sorry to hear that."

"Oh, it'll either work out or I'll go somewhere else."

"Do you know; is there any work around here?" Tom asked.

"What kind of work?"

"Something I can walk away from in a couple of days. I just need to make enough to buy some supplies and get back on the trail."

"You mind doing dishes?"

"Not at all."

"Good, I work at Midnight Bar and Grill. All the locals go there."

"Midnight Bar. I guess you guys stay open every night until midnight?"

Amber laughed softly. "No. I don't know why they call it that. We close at eleven-thirty on weeknights and one-thirty on Saturdays. We're closed on Sunday."

Tom chuckled. "I read there was a youth hostel in town. Do you know where it is?"

Amber's lips began to twitch a little and she shook her head. "You don't want to stay there, Tom."

"Why not? I've stayed in other ones. They seemed okay."

"It's a dump. An embarrassment to our town. Listen, I start work at five o'clock. If you like, we can go to my condo. We have enough time. You can wash your clothes, shower, and shave that shabby beard of yours. My neighbor cuts hair for a living. If we're lucky, I think she has today off. She could give you a quick clip and then I can take you to the bar and introduce you to the owner."

"That would be great, but I don't want to put you out of the way."

Amber gave him a quick glimpse as she put both hands on the steering wheel, zipping around another sharp turn. The tires squealed. "We like helping hikers up here. This isn't my first time helping, and it won't be my last."

When they got to the condo, Tom liked what he saw. Thank God she didn't have a bunch of frilly things around. It wasn't cluttered, and she kept it clean. She had some nice photos on the walls. They were all outdoor photos, with no people and no buildings. There was one that stole the show. A large spiderweb in the foreground with detailed microdots of moisture on the threads. In the background, there were out-of-focus red and green leaves. "You've got some really nice art."

"Thanks, I like to think of myself as an amateur photographer."

Tom's mouth dropped open. "No way. You shot these photos?" Amber nodded.

"Very impressive."

Tom walked over to the other side of the room. Books lined several shelves. Most were about photography and there were a few novels. Tom smiled, realizing she had only one self-help book: *I'm OK, You're OK,* by a psychiatrist named Thomas Harris.

"Let me show you where the washer and dryer are."

"My shower is in the bedroom. I assume you want to wash everything, so here," she took a robe off a hanger, "you can wear this."

"Thanks."

"You get started and I'll check and see if my neighbor is around."

It was a short, white, waffle-weaved bathrobe. Simple and sturdy. Tom took his sweet time in the shower. The hot water and steam never felt so good. He celebrated, soaping up his body and hair. It felt so good; he thought about doing it again when he heard Amber calling him through the door.

"What's that?"

Amber cracked the bathroom door and steam began to ease out.

"I said, time to get your haircut."

"OK, would you hand me a towel?" He stuck his hand out, opening and closing it. Amber handed him a small washcloth.

"Very funny, Amber." Actually, he did think it was.

She cracked up as she handed him a regular towel. He dried off behind the curtain, wrapped the towel around his waist, and stepped out. Amber was leaning against the sink. After a short minute, she left.

"While you get your hair cut, I'll fix us some food."

Amber's neighbor was a nice, pleasant woman in her late fifties. She wore a tie-dyed T-shirt and faded blue jeans. She was fast to tell Tom she was the local historian.

"Do you like your hair long, or since you are on the trail, maybe you want it short?" she asked.

"Let's go with short. And also, can you buzz off my beard?"

"Maybe keep your mustache. I can just trim it up a little, see if you like it?"

Tom nodded. "So, tell me about Waynesboro."

"Waynesboro has been here since 1794."

God could not have made a more monotone, soft voice. *I love history, but the people who tell it are always boring.*

"It was named after a Revolutionary War general named Anthony Wayne; better known as 'Mad Anthony' due to his fiery personality."

Her story went on and on. He was just about to fall asleep when she finished his haircut and started on his beard. She was a short, stout woman with a bowling ball head. She kept a cigarette in her mouth at all times. A chain smoker. She also had yellow, nicotine-stained fingertips. She was sweet and had a kind, loving spirit. *Bet she was rich with friends.* She backed away and called Amber for a look. They both smiled.

"You look like a different man," Amber said, patting her friend on the back.

"How much do I owe you?" Tom asked.

"Nonsense; any friend of Amber's is a friend of mine, sweetheart."

After the stylist left, Tom and Amber enjoyed a turkey sandwich, corn chips, and a beer. A nice cold beer.

Chapter Six
Appalachian Trail, Virginia
1974
Revenge, Sweet Revenge

Amber's boss was sitting in a booth doing paperwork. He was an older man in his mid-sixties, with an alcoholic reddish flush about his nose and cheeks.

"Have a seat, young man. Name's Gus."

"Tom Hunt."

"What brings you here?"

"I'm hiking the trail."

Something crashed noisily to the floor. It was a whole pile of dishes dropped by a now-frightened waitress. Tom stood up to help.

"Keep your seat, Tom. Let her clean up her own damn mess."

Tom slid uneasily back into the booth. The upholstery was old and worn out. Was the color originally dark green and over the years faded into a fern-green color? Or had it started off black? Didn't matter. It was just plain old ugly. The walls were lined with photos of local sports teams and their cheerleading squads. Like the battered old booth, they too looked outdated.

"Amber tells me you might have a job for me."

"The only thing I have right now is a part-time dishwasher."

Tom nodded. "What's it pay?"

"Well, the minimum wage is $1.60 an hour, but all I can offer is a buck an hour. Cash under the table."

"OK, I'll take it. When can I start?"

"Tomorrow night. You get the five to close shift."

They shook hands. Tom could see the waitress was still cleaning up her mess as he went to the bar. "Come Together" by the Beatles was playing from a nice 8-track system behind the bar.

Amber served beers and talked to the locals as she worked her way over to Tom.

"How did it go?" she asked.

"Good enough. The pay is pretty low, but I start tomorrow night." She smiled.

"How much for a cold draft beer?"

"Fifty cents."

"What do you recommend?"

"We have PBR on draft. That's good."

"Sold." Tom nodded. "By the way, do you have any Rolling Stones?"

"Sure. How about 'Satisfaction'?"

"No, too overplayed. How about, 'Get Off My Cloud'?"

"Cool," Amber said and pulled out a beer.

Tom admired the tall, frosted glass with a two-inch head of foam on it. His tastebuds screamed with pleasure and then he concentrated on the delicate smoothness of the brew.

Two men approached the bar with an air of arrogance. *Holy shit.* Tom recognized them instantly. It was the gangly guy, Texas, and the bald, bearded Goliath dude, Bama. They were standing only a few feet away. *Wow, they don't recognize me.* Tom's fresh haircut, shave, and clean clothes were a good disguise. He was a new man.

Tom wanted to slam his mug into Bama's face, but he held back. If he missed, he would probably be the one heading to the hospital. No, he needed to plot his revenge.

The two thugs took their beers to a table in the far corner. He waved to Amber.

"Amber, do you know those two guys you just served?"

"No, but they come in every now and then. They stay mostly to themselves." Amber wiped the bar countertop with a rag. "I know they are cheap tippers."

"Which door did they come in?"

"I saw them come in from the back."

"If it's okay with you, I'll head back to your place and wait for you."

"You don't need to wait to get in; I have a key under the front doormat."

Tom laughed. "Wow, if I was a thief, I would have never thought to look there."

Downing his beer, Tom got up and put down a couple of bucks. "You don't have to do that," Amber protested.

"I thought you said you were hurting for cash. Besides, I want to."

Smiling, Amber got back to work. She pulled on a wooden keg handle. A stream of golden liquid splashed into a cold mug. Tom waved goodbye and walked out the back door.

There was one spotlight on the roof of the bar. A quarter moon shone dimly. Tom was looking for a good place to ambush the two thugs. They had left him for dead on the trail! *Those bastards are going to pay.* He spied on a large dumpster. *Perfect!* The blind side of it was the perfect place to hide. Now he needed to find a good weapon. He saw a baseball bat hanging on a gun rack in a pickup truck. The door to the truck was unlocked. Looking around to make sure no one was watching; he took the bat. *Sweet, a 34" Louisville slugger.* In small towns, few lock their doors, some don't even lock their house.

Tom squatted behind the dumpster, preparing for what might be a long wait. Every time people came out of the bar laughing and talking loudly, Tom would tense up and then realize it was not them. An hour passed. Tom thought about tossing the bat and walking away when the door popped open again and there they were.

Bama was walking closest to Tom. He gripped the bat tightly. His heart was pounding, and he was sweating even though it was a cold night. *Patience.* The thugs were taking their sweet time.

They were oblivious to Tom. He stepped out, swinging as hard as he could at Bama's knee. He heard bones crack. Bama fell to the ground, screaming with pain, rolling back and forth, holding his knee. Texas pulled out his gun, but Tom had already cocked his bat. The bat smashed Texas' gun hand, sending the gun flying. Tom swung again, hitting Texas in the jaw. The bottom half dislocated and hung next to his ear. Teeth went sailing. Texas dropped to the ground, knocked out cold. Bama was still rolling on the ground, holding his knee. Tom unleashed another swing, smashing the other knee. Tom held the bat over Bama.

"What do you want?" Bama cried. "Here, you want money?" Pulling out a roll of cash, he tossed it to Tom. "There, there's two grand."

Picking it up, Tom held it in his hand. "Fuck you, man. You recognize me?"

"Yeah, you're that SOB we found on the trail."

The back door of the bar banged open. Amber was bringing out some trash. She saw Tom standing over the two men. She dropped the trash and ran out to him. "My God, what happened?"

"These two thugs almost killed me. I ran across them on the trail. They're drug mules." Out of breath, Tom tried to explain further. "They drugged me up and left me as an OD case for somebody to find."

Amber's face flushed white as she looked at the carnage of the gangly man's face. She whispered, "Get out of here. Go back to my place and wait for me. Take the bat with you and get rid of it."

"What are you going to do?"

"I said, go! I'll clean things up here."

Tom started running, holding the bat as he sprinted past his victims.

*

Tom tossed the bat down a sewer drain. He heard and then saw a cop car coming full blast with his blues flashing. Tom jolted and stopped running. He walked casually into a pay phone booth next to the town drugstore, but the police car turned sharply toward the bar.

He thought about the last time he called Callie. It was months ago, and she sounded colder than usual. She told Tom how tired she was of him being gone. He put a dime in the slot and dialed "0".

"Operator, I want to make a collect call." He gave her Callie's phone number. Excitement grew as he listened to a few rings.

"Hello?" Hearing her voice brought back a flood of memories. Tom could picture her eyes. God, how he wanted to hold her.

"You have a collect call from Tom; will you accept it?"

There was a short pause before she gave a stern, "No," and hung up. Tom's stomach twisted. He put the receiver down and stood there in shock. He felt for another dime and asked the operator to call Alfred's number. It took four rings for Alfred to pick up.

"Hey, Tom."

"Alfred, what's going on with Callie? I just tried to call her, and she wouldn't even take my call." There was a long pause, and Tom got antsy. He fidgeted with the phone cord, wrapping it around his index finger. "Alfred, what's going on?"

"Tom, you have been gone a long time and Callie is a damn good-looking woman."

"I know that."

"Well, what the hell do you think happened?"

Biting his lower lip, Tom asked, "Who? Who is it?"

"What difference does it make, Tom? She's moved on with her life."

Tom was caught flat-footed. He didn't know what to say. "I'm coming down to see her."

"No! She knew that's what you'd say, and she doesn't want to see you. Don't come."

Tom's eyes swelled with tears. "I can't believe it; Callie is gone."

"Listen, Tom, since you have been gone, you have written two postcards and called her just once."

"I know, but I told her I would be back… She promised she would wait for me." Tom was still struggling to get his breath.

"Who the hell is it, Alfred? Do I know the guy?"

"It doesn't matter, Tom."

"God damn it, who?"

"It's Jack."

"Jack? Not my fraternity brother, Jack? Not one of my best friends, Jack? No, I don't believe it. Hell, he hiked with us. No! Not that Jack?"

"Yes, that Jack. And, to tell you the truth, Tom, Jack, and Callie are much more suited for each other than you and Callie."

"What the hell does that mean?"

"It means they both want a big family, lots of kids, a house with a white picket fence, two dogs, to belong to a Baptist church, and to live in a small town where everybody knows them. She'll teach in the local grammar school, and he'll be the president of some bank. Everything that you would find boring, and you know it. You're just pissed right now because your ego got crushed, but if you gave it half a second thought, you would know I'm right."

*

Tom tried to focus, but everything was a blur. His arms and legs felt heavy as he hung up the receiver. *What a fuckin' night.*

Amber arrived home at two a.m. She had been questioned by the police trying to get to the bottom of the bloody attack on the two men behind the bar. She got a lot more information than she gave. The police wrote it up as a mob-on-mob attack. Both victims were sent to the hospital. Texas was taken to intensive care and would need immediate surgery on his jaw. Amber told Tom that

Mississippi wouldn't stop screaming about how he was going to get even with the SOB who did this to him.

"Tom, you got to get out of town as soon as it gets to be daylight."

"What about work? I just told Gus I would take the job." Tom didn't care diddly-squat about those two thugs; he was thinking about his loss of Callie.

"You hang around here, Tom, and somebody is going to kill you."

Dropping his head into his hands, Tom agreed. "Yeah, I guess it is time to move on."

"I heard the cops talking about those two guys you roughed up. Tom, they are known soldiers in the Burno family mafia out of Philadelphia. Their capo—"

"Capo? What's a capo?"

"The soldiers report to a capo, which is like a captain in the military."

"I think I met their capo." Tom described the guy.

"Yeah, I think I have seen him at the bar every once in a while. Anyway, he isn't going to sit around and let some college kid take out his men. The guy whose knees you took out wouldn't give the police your description, but I am sure he knows, and he is going to tell his buddies." Tom's eyes were swollen and red.

"Tom, you better get your rest now; tomorrow, I'll drive you up to the trail."

Tom tossed and turned, thinking about Callie, the first time he saw her, the first time they made love, the good times they had.

*

The next morning, it was another cloudy, rainy day, but that would play well for Tom's escape. People don't like to tramp around in bad weather if they don't have to, especially on mushy mountain trails.

Amber gave Tom access to her kitchen pantry so he could stock up. He took her granola bars, Ritz crackers, cheese straws, peanut butter, Hamburger Helper–even though he wouldn't have any ground meat–and some small cans of Spam.

She drove Tom as close as she could to the trail and parked her car. Turning and looking at him, she said, "When you get on the trail, don't stop at any of the towns until you are far away from here." She leaned in and gave him a soft kiss on the cheek.

"Maybe I can stop by here on the way back."

"No! Don't ever show up in Waynesboro again. The mafia has a long memory."

Tom reached into his coat pocket and pulled out the roll of money that Alabama had thrown at him. He kept a few hundred dollars for himself and handed her the rest.

"There should be nearly two thousand."

"Where did you get this?"

"That guy I whacked on the knees threw it at me, hoping I would stop." Tom explained, "Want you to have it. You said that you needed money, or you would have to move. This ought to take care of your bills while you get back on your feet. Take care, Amber."

Tom got out of the car and looked through the window at her. Smiling, she revved the engine of her Mustang. Tom backed away. "You see, you do like attention."

Chapter Seven
Appalachian Trail, Virginia
1974
Running Hard

Tom caught up with Pat at Calf Mountain Shelter. Right away, he told him about what happened with the mafia assholes in Waynesboro. Pat was duly impressed and understood Tom's fear. They didn't waste any time. They hiked nonstop until sunset.

The next day, they decided to split up and let Pat take the lead. The mafia ruffians would be looking for Tom, not Pat. If Pat saw something suspicious, he would circle back and warn Tom. They plotted where each would camp for the next four nights.

Tom was to avoid all shelters, make no fires, or use a flashlight, and he was to sleep without setting up a tent, even if it was raining. Above all, no towns until this was over. They would reunite one mile north of Rod Hollow Shelter.

Virginia has more than five hundred miles of the AT, the most in the country. But the bad guys didn't have to cover five hundred miles. They had a general idea of where Tom was. If the net was big enough, they could capture Tom, torture him, and kill him.

The idea of being tortured and murdered kept Tom moving and on the lookout. He would avoid anybody that was on the trail and trust no one. By the fourth day, Tom was worn out and had depleted most of his supplies. This was the heavy price of scrambling out of town in a hurry.

It had been another hard day of hiking and Tom was done. He had Hamburger Helper and a handful of crushed-up noodles. Placing the noodles in a pan of cold water, he added the contents of the box. The noodles eventually softened, and Tom slurped the gruel down. *I wish I could make a damn fire. A warm dinner sure would be nice. Trail dining sucks.*

It was a good sign that Pat hadn't circled back. Maybe the mafia didn't have the spare men to go searching the forest. Maybe. OK, that was Tom's wishful prayer.

He was looking for some good bushes to crawl into or a log to get behind when he saw a cabin in the distance. Tom approached carefully along a sloping gravel driveway. *What the hell is a cabin doing here?*

Black and gray plumes came out of the fieldstone chimney. *Somebody's here.* It looked dry and warm. A dark green Jeep was beside the cabin. A woman was smoking and rocking back and forth. He was too far away to tell much about her. Edging his way to the back of the cabin, he listened for more sounds. Nada. He was certain there was no one else, so he walked out into the open.

"Hello," Tom offered with a friendly smile.

She didn't reply right off. Directly, she waved him over. "You want a smoke? Marlboro's what I got."

"No, but thanks anyway." *I wish it was pot. So much for avoiding people.*

She pointed to the old-timey cane rocker next to her. "Have a seat."

She was made to look wise and knowing by the fine wrinkles in the corners of her startling blue, almost azure, eyes. They were like none he had seen before. She looked to be in her mid-forties and had dirty blonde hair tied into a ponytail. Her eyes were mysterious and seeking, but that aspect was balanced by a festive playfulness, a lightness of being, so to speak. A light brown, almost tan, mole lay between her right eyebrow and eye. Her nose had been broken, noticeably so. *Had she been abused sometime in her life? Or perhaps she had just played sports in her youth?*

"I wasn't expecting a log cabin out here in the middle of nowhere."

"This cabin has been in my family for generations, and it is right up against the George Washington National Forest boundary line. At one time, it was a logging lodge, but it was eventually more or less spoiled. They cleared tracks of land. Hell, they scalped the forest. What you see now," she swept her hand, "is a new forest."

"Really, that's interesting. I wish my family had something like this."

She was wearing bell-bottom jeans and a University of Virginia Cavaliers charcoal-colored sweatshirt.

"My name's Tom Hunt."

She took a long draw on her cigarette and crushed it out on the worn-gray wooden porch planks. "Nice name, Tom. Mine's Gail Roberson."

They were slowly rocking back and forth. Tom liked that she could sit in silence without discomfort. She would be an excellent trail mate.

"Where ya from, Tom?"

"Atlanta. And you?"

"Born in Charlottesville and still live there. I come up here to get away from it all." There was a certain sadness about her tone. Or perhaps that was just the sound of boredom.

A faint hint of daylight remained. Something scurried across the gravel driveway. It was a big fat raccoon.

"That trash panda is a smart little scavenger."

Tom laughed. "I've never heard it called that before."

"He eats out of my trash cans. I named him Bandit. He can open locks that most people couldn't get into."

Bandit headed into the forest with a half-eaten orange dripping out of his mouth.

"He sure isn't shy," Tom said.

"Actually, when I leave, I put out a couple of different fruits and a few eggs."

"No wonder he hangs around."

"Yeah, I have a soft spot for all the creatures that come around."

Hmm, am I included in that list of creatures?

"So, what kind of work do you do?" Tom asked.

Gail stopped rocking. She rolled her eyes downward and cocked her head back so she could see Tom. She hesitated for a bit. "Well, if you call going to fundraisers or auctions to buy incredibly expensive art or throwing lavish parties for your husband's business contacts a job, then I have one. I guess you could say I am a professional socialite."

"Sounds lavish."

"Well, Tom, there is rich, then there is very rich, and then there is my husband's crowd of eff-you rich."

She held up her hand, showing off a huge diamond ring. It was beyond ostentatious. It sparkled. *Jesus.*

"Damn, what a stunning ring."

"The experts say it is perfect on all 4 Cs," she said.

"And what are the 4 Cs?"

"It doesn't matter. Just know it's flawless and very expensive."

"I'm sorry. I didn't mean to stare. But I wonder why you would wear it out here?"

"Well, why not? If I lose it, I'll just get another one, probably bigger."

Wow, that's crazy. "What exactly does your husband do?"

"He buys companies, tears them apart, and then sells them." She sounded cold and hard.

"I take it you disapprove."

"Me? Why should I disapprove of ruining thousands of people's lives so we can be rich?" She stood up. "Would you like a drink?"

"Yes."

Gail was about 5'6" and country good-looking. "Why don't you come on inside?"

It was far from rustic inside. The solid wooden columns, recessed lighting, a long wood slab table made of an amazing and probably quite rare zebrano, an exotic hardwood, and matching benches were all presented in the spacious living room. The floor throughout was a light marble of differing hues. There was an assortment of University of Virginia paraphernalia, a solid walnut box with the university emblem engraved on it, Virginia Cavaliers tumbler glasses, and a large drawing of the university from 1819 on the wall next to the dining table.

"Wow! Your place is incredible."

"I should have added to my list of jobs, decorator. We have three houses, but this is my favorite. I like it the most because it is my retreat, and it's simple."

This is simple. I'd hate to see what you call eloquent.

"Warren, that's my husband, won't set foot in it. He's not the outdoor type."

"Did you say three houses?"

She nodded. "One in the Bahamas, one in Charlottesville, and this one."

She had a cold bottle of vodka in the freezer. Apparently she had already knocked out a good bit. "I don't have anything to mix with this except ice and olives; is that okay?"

"Sounds good to me."

She poured generous drinks, very generous. Leading Tom to the den, she put another log on the fire and moseyed over to the antique brown leather couch facing the local fieldstone fireplace.

"You say this used to be a railroad shelter?"

"No, a logger lodge."

"Oh, yeah."

"Of course, we changed it after I inherited it. As I said, it has been in my family for a long time. Maybe that's another reason why I love it up here. It reminds me of my grandfather. He was a salt-of-the-earth kind of guy. Papa didn't get caught up playing all the social games. Money was important, but money for money's sake was for fools. I remember Papa quoting some philosopher. I forgot his name, but he would say, 'Gail, wealth is like seawater: The more we drink, the thirstier we become, and the same is true of fame.'" She half laughed at the memory. "Papa was always full of good advice."

"Sounds like a wise man."

A set of photos was displayed neatly on the coffee table. "Your family?"

"Yes."

"You have two children?"

"Yes, the one on the right, Jane, is the oldest. She's graduating from my alma mater this year."

"The University of Virginia?"

"Yes, what gave it away?" She laughed. "The one on the left, Hope, is in her second year at Virginia Tech. The little traitor."

Tom studied the two girls. They were both beautiful, but Jane looked just like her mom. There was also a picture of Gail's wedding. The couple was standing next to a seven-tier laced wedding cake with a gold monogram. He was a short man, no taller than Gail, heavyset, and he looked very serious. No smile, and he had dark-rimmed tinted glasses hiding his eyes. Gail was all smiles and looked stunning in her antique silk-embroidered wedding dress. *I wonder how these two got together.*

"You have a beautiful family."

She gave a short nod and took a big swig.

It was a cozy afternoon in a warm cabin, and they spent the better part of it talking about the type of things Gail did when she was up there. She was crazy about kayaking, and there were serious rapids nearby. No television, but she did have music. There was a shelf stacked with records. Tom started thumbing through them; Diana Ross and the Supremes, B. J. Thomas, Neil Diamond, The Carpenters, and a number of other similar artists. No Beatle, no Stones, and no Pink Floyd.

"But then there's my favorite pastime, Tom."

Gail gestured for Tom to follow her to a small room with some sort of an electronic device that looked somewhat ominous sitting in the corner.

"Your office?"

"Yes. Do you know what that machine over there is?"

"A radio?"

"Yes, a ham radio. I'm addicted to this thing. I got my operator's license years ago. It's actually my only source of communication when I stay up here. But lots of people around here use them."

"What about your husband? Doesn't he want you to have a phone in case something happens?"

"I have another unit in our Charlottesville home. I taught him how to use it. I have a special channel just for him."

"By the way, do you know what chatter I have been picking up today?" she continued.

"Not a clue."

"You're him, aren't you, Tom?"

Tom didn't answer.

"You're the guy that a lot of people want to find. The chatter says that someone has put a reward out on your head, ten thousand dollars." Cocking her eyebrows high, she continued, "Wow, that would buy a brand-new car."

Tom thought about bolting. Or perhaps tie her up and take her Jeep. "So, what are you going to do?" he asked.

"Don't worry, I don't need a new car; I have three already." Gail picked up a pack of smokes off her office desk and pulled one out. She played with it for a minute but tossed it aside. "Let's go back to the couch." Once settled, she asked, "Why are they chasing you and who are they?"

Tom told his story from the time he was captured on the trail until he sent the bastards to the hospital.

"And who are they?" she asked.

"They are with the Burno family."

"The mafia family out of Philadelphia?"

"Yes."

"That's interesting."

Tom's mouth gaped open, and his eyes widened. *Interesting? That's not what I'd call it.*

"The Burno family is well known for bookmaking, gambling, and extortion, but their boss, Angelo 'the Gentle Don' Burno, refuses to deal with drugs. It's probably just a matter of time before the money lures him in, but for now, Don Angelo, like Paul Castello, wants nothing to do with it."

"Who's Paul?"

"You are a babe in the woods. Paul Castello, the don of the Gambino family, believes the future is in white-collar crimes. Paul believes that drugs will be the end of the mafia if they get involved."

"How do you know all this about the Burno and Gambino families?"

"I know Don Angelo personally. My husband has done a lot of business with him. Money laundering, to be specific. He's like Castello. He's a family operation."

Gail was slurring her words, and she seemed very relaxed. He could only guess how many drinks she had before he showed up.

"Let's have another drink." She held out her hand for Tom. He slid his hand comfortably into hers and pulled her up. They went to the kitchen, hand in hand the whole way. Before releasing her grip, she looked at him long and intensely. Her neck and cheeks blushed pink. Tom took a gulp of his drink.

"Well, I have to say, Tom, when you screw up, you really screw up."

Tom's throat tightened. He felt he was on the verge of puking.

*

Gail invited Tom to stay the night and offered to drive him north the next day, far enough to go beyond the mafia net closing in on him. Tom was more than happy to take her up on both offers.

The spacious guest bedroom had a fireplace similar to the one in the living room, but smaller. It was already set up and ready to go. Tom lit the fire and crawled into bed. It was past midnight when he heard the door open. Gail was wearing a silk nightshirt, slit high on the sides, and nothing else. She was quite beautiful, standing provocatively against the glow of the fire.

Her nightie slipped to the floor with a little swish. She kissed him hotly and slid into bed. She let her hair down and swept it slowly across his chest and then lowered herself down... He had her three times that night.

Tom forgot all about the mafia and what they would do to him if he were caught. He was free of worries; not even Callie concerned him tonight.

The next morning, Gail was already up and dressed when he woke up. She had switched sweatshirts; now she was wearing an orange Cavaliers fleece. She was sitting back in a chair, holding a big cup of coffee.

"Good morning, sleepyhead. This will get you going. Hope you like it black."

Tom rubbed his eyes before taking the coffee. He had always been slow to wake up in the mornings.

"Tom, we need to get going as soon as possible."

There was no time for small talk. No reflecting on the night before. No real feeling of an emotional bond growing. Just the cold reality that he needed to get his ass out of there.

"What are you hearing on the radio?"

"They are close, Tom. They'll be on us soon and I need to get to a pay phone."

"Pay phone?"

"Yes, I am going to call in a favor… I am going to call Don Burno."

Tom jumped out of bed naked and grabbed her arms.

"What? Are you crazy? They will know exactly where I am!"

"Trust me, Tom. I am going to tell him that you are a relative, that you are family, and why you did what you did."

"I don't think that's a good idea, Gail."

"Two things will happen. First, he will treasure the idea that my husband and I will owe him a favor, and trust me, mafia bosses never forget who owes them favors. And second, when he finds out drugs were involved without his knowledge, he'll be furious. Someone will pay for it."

"I don't know." Tom backed away from her and picked his underwear off the floor. "If it doesn't work, and he doesn't call off his dogs, I am dead."

"Tom, if he doesn't call off his dogs, we are both dead. They will kill me for helping you. Now, get dressed. I'll see you in the kitchen."

The fear of torture grabbed his gut, deep. He scrambled down to the kitchen. Gail was packing a couple of boxes. Old lamps, dishes, coffee mugs, serving platters, dish towels, and Tupperware. Several old rugs were stacked up next to the door.

"What's all this for?"

"I've been putting these aside for Goodwill. But in the meantime, they'll be camouflaged for you. I'm gonna put you on the floor in the back and stack all of this on top of you so the inglorious bastards can't spot you."

She picked up one of the boxes and strolled briskly out the already open door. Tom picked up the rugs and immediately smelled a strong, musky odor. *Oh well...*

Gail's Jeep was made for rough terrain, but it was not made to hide someone. It was a two-door with bucket seats and a small bench seat in the back. The Jeep's roof, when it was covered as it was now, was a snap-on made of black vinyl.

"Get on the floor in the back." She covered him with the rugs and then the boxes.

"You really think this will work?"

"You got a better idea? If you try to walk out of here, I guarantee they will find you."

"I know I gotta run, but I don't know where I am going. I'm just running."

Tom was curled up on the floor and already uncomfortable as hell. The stink of the rugs was overbearing. He was well hidden. If no one started poking around.

Chapter Eight
Appalachian Trail, Virginia
1974
Go Your Own Way

Laying on the floorboard of a Jeep riding over a rough gravel road with Texas-sized potholes sucked. The vibrations alone were enough, but the jostling and jolting were aggravating as hell. A mattress would have been nice. The Jeep sounded like an industrial meat grinder as it hauled ass down the road. *Her freakin' shocks must be worn out.*

They turned onto a paved road and the bumpety-bump ceased. Gail pulled into a Texaco station. An eager teenage boy immediately ran out and started pumping gas, cleaning the windshield, and checking the oil. She found a pay phone and called Don Burno. It was short and to the point. He appreciated what she told him and promised to stop his boys from harming Tom.

Gail paid, thanked the young boy, and took off.

"We're lucky, Tom."

"What happened?"

"Don Burno listened to what I had to say. His underboss, Maxwell, is at his farm this week."

The loud whistling sound of the Jeep drowned out her voice.

"What did you say, Gail? I can't hear back here."

She shouted, "I said, the call went well. The underboss is on the way to help us. He's at his farm about forty miles from my cabin. He'll stop the search."

The road was smoother, but it was still cramped and smelly. There was a fork in the road. Gail slowed down and then took the fork to the right. "We're going around the mountain, Tom. It's a little more curvy than the rest, but safer."

Great, time to get carsick. It wasn't long before Tom felt the car slow down.

"Tom, don't move a muscle."

Gail slowed down. Two men stood in the middle of the road, waving for her to stop. She turned up her radio. Lynyrd Skynyrd's "Free Bird" was blaring. She put on a pair of Ray-Ban aviator mirrored sunglasses. Tom heard her roll down her window.

"You boys need some help?" she hollered with a friendly fake smile.

"Turn off the engine!" A large man stepped up to the side of the Jeep. He had a large nose, and mahogany brown eyes, and walked with a slight limp. His reptilian stare screamed evil. Loud music flooded out of the Jeep.

"What's that?"

Evil eyes barked, "I said, turn the damn jeep off!"

She nervously turned down the radio. "What's going on?"

"Don't make me say it again, lady."

"OK, okay." She turned off the engine.

"Are you out here alone?"

"Yes, I own a cabin up here."

The man eyed the back of the Jeep.

"What's all this crap back here?" Evil eyes pointed to the boxes.

"I'm taking this stuff to Goodwill."

"Have you seen a young man? Brown hair, mustache, about 6'2" or so."

"No."

"Get out of the Jeep."

"What? No way."

The man opened her door, grabbed her arm, pulled her out roughly, and shoved her hard to the ground. Her sunglasses spun off and skittered across the blacktop.

"Shut up, bitch."

Yelling to the sky, the nasty man said, "Mister, don't make me have to do this… I'm going to hurt this woman if you don't come out right now."

There was no reply. Evil eyes nodded to the guy with the shotgun. His buddy, who was smoking a cigar, pointed his shotgun five feet away from Gail. Dust spiraled upward and gravel splattered her legs. Gail screamed. She clutched at her face in shock. Tom scrambled up from beneath the boxes. "OK. All right already. I'm coming."

"Well, well, well… look here what we found. Get your puny ass out here."

Tom moved very slowly out of the Jeep. He stood innocently with his hands held high. Out of nowhere, evil eyes slammed his fist into Tom's solar plexus. Tom grunted loudly and fell to his knees, gasping for breath.

"That was for my friend who got his knees destroyed by a baseball bat." He smashed his boot into Tom's face. "And that is for my friend, who will drink from a straw for the next few months."

Blood poured from Tom's nose and mouth. Everything blurred. He partially pushed himself up, but caved to the ground and was down for the count. When he came to, there were several more badass guys, including the capo, Kentucky.

"He's coming around, Zack," evil eyes yelled out.

So, it's capo Zack. Yep, square jaw, cleft chin, salt-and-pepper hair, and a buckskin coat. That's him all right. The son-of-a bitch.

"Don't ever use my name again, dickhead. Only nicknames!" Zack said harshly. "Shit, why don't you tell the guy my full name and while you're at it, give him my phone number and address? Dumb shit."

The others stared at the ground. Zack waved at a guy with long, straight raven-black hair and mahogany skin. "Blackfoot, bring that bitch over here."

Zack grabbed the hair on top of Tom's head and roughly pulled him up. "This here's a genuine Native American Indian, well at least he's twenty percent. Care to guess what tribe? At any rate, he's the best at what he does."

Blackfoot turned to face Gail. Her clothes were dirty and the little bit of mascara that she wore was smeared.

"Are you okay?" Gail asked.

Tom nodded. "How about you?"

"I'm okay."

"Yeah, you may be now, but let me introduce you to Blackfoot. You see, he has a real chip on his shoulder about how his forefathers were treated. At least that's my theory. He has this thing about getting even." Zack put his arm around Blackfoot. "So, brother, which one of these two would you like to torture first?"

Blackfoot locked eyes with each of them. He rubbed his jaw with great consideration.

"For God's sake, dude, we don't have all day." Zack pulled out a silver dollar from his pants pocket. "Here, I'll make it easy for you. Heads, the woman, tails, the dude."

He tossed the coin into the air and let it hit the ground. They both bent over. It was heads. "Ha, whatcha got in mind for this sweet little bitch?"

"*Hmm.* Let me think."

Zack rubbed his hands together. "How about we make a small fire… and then… we make her sit that little penis flytrap of hers on hot coals?"

Zack gave a hideous laugh and balled his fists. Blackfoot rubbed his jaw. Zack stopped celebrating his clever idea. "OK, how about we tie her up and throw knives at her?"

"*Hmm.*" There was a short pause. "No."

"Hell's bells, then tell me what you want to do." Blackfoot stood over Gail, reached down, and felt one of her tits.

"I get it; you want to rape her?"

"No, I want her tits."

Zack frowned. "What do you mean? You just want to play with her tits?"

"No, I want her tits. I want to make tobacco pouches out of them."

"Wow," Zack shook his head, "I didn't see that one coming."

Tom struggled to his knees. "Listen, she had nothing to do with this. I forced her to drive me. I told her that I would kill her if she didn't."

"Oh really? Well, I'll take that into great consideration." Zack paused for two seconds. "Nope, that doesn't change a fuckin' thing."

The men laughed sadistically, waiting to see what Blackfoot would do. Blackfoot ripped off Gail's shirt, grabbed her bra with one hand, and yanked it off. Gail was topless in one smooth motion in the blink of an eye. "You see," Blackfoot slung the bra down, "those are nice and firm; they are the perfect size for tobacco pouches."

Blackfoot slapped her hard across the face. She went limp. He grabbed her left breast and put a cold steel blade to her chest and started to slice downward.

Bam! Bam! Bam! A Land Rover blistered past, a big pistol sticking out the window. Guns and rifles were drawn.

Blackfoot shoved Gail away and dove to the ground.

"Don't fire!" Zack shouted. "I think that's..." He squinted his eyes tightly, "that's one of our guys driving... and the guy next to him is... I'll be damned." He stood up and waved to them that all was clear.

They screeched to a halt. Four men got out of the vehicle. "Stop everything," demanded a short little stump of a man. His face resembled an old Boston terrier, with large, almond-shaped eyes, pointy ears, and a red-veined pug-nose.

"Jesus," Blackfoot whispered, "why is Stumpy here?"

"Hello, Gail."

Gail nodded. "Hello, Maxwell."

Through clenched teeth, Maxwell said, "Blackfoot, give her your damn coat."

Blackfoot nervously fumbled with the zipper and then wrapped his coat around Gail. He backed away from Zack. Maxwell's jaw was twitching. He was furious.

"So, what dumbass thought it would be a good idea to take Ms. Roberson as a prisoner?"

"You know her, boss?" Zack asked.

Maxwell studied his face. "Do you have any idea who her husband is, capo?"

"No, sir."

"He is a consigliere for Don Angelo, and he and his entire family have full protection. This man here—"

"I reported what he did," Zack defended.

"I know. But this young man is a cousin of hers."

Such a *nice touch, Gail.*

"So, I don't care if he cuts your balls off. Her family is protected."

"But—"

"Protected means fucking protected!" The veins in Maxwell's neck were bulging, and he was now spraying spittle with every word.

"But—"

Maxwell threw up his hands for Zack to shut up. "They," he pointed at Gail and Tom, "are not the only reason I came down here."

"I know, boss… I'm bringing you money at the end of this month," Zack swallowed hard, "and it will be considerably more than usual."

"Oh, and what did you do differently that got you so much money?"

"Different? Nothing different, just more than usual."

"So what business are you most profitable with… porn, loansharking, gambling, bars?"

"All of them were up this quarter, boss."

"Really?"

"It was a killer quarter."

Maxwell looked into Zack's eyes, smiling, and he straightened the capo's collar. "That's good, Zack." His voice hardened. "Except I know you are a lying piece of scum."

"What?"

"You heard me, Zack. You are a lying piece of scum. You got more money all right. You got it by breaking a family law."

"I don't know what you are talking about, boss?"

Maxwell ripped out his pistol. Bam! He shot Zack smack dab in the middle of his forehead. Strangely, it looked like a third eye had gone horribly wrong. Blood splattered everywhere. He was dead before he hit the ground. Not missing a beat, Maxwell turned to the others. "The Don will decide who your next capo will be. Don't make the same mistake as he did. No drugs in our family, you understand?"

"Yes, sir," they said in feared unison.

"Now clean up this mess."

"Hey boss," Blackfoot yelled out, "what do we do with the woman and her cousin?"

"Jesus, I'm surrounded by an ocean of stupidity. Let 'em go!" Maxwell looked at Gail, smiled assuredly, and gave her a mock salute. "See you soon."

She nodded back, finally grinning. "See ya soon, Maxwell."

Chapter Nine
Charlottesville, Va.
1974
Racin' Against Time

Bright red blood splattered Gail's shirt. Her hands were mud-red. Tom pulled a rag from the glove box. She was cut pretty badly, a gash across the top of her left breast. "Here, put this on it. Press down hard!"

"I'm okay, Tom."

"Bullshit, you need a doctor. And I mean now. Where's the closest ER?"

Gail said nothing. Perhaps she realized the depth of trouble she was in. She was breathing deeply through her nose to lessen the pain. "Go to Sentara Martha Jefferson Hospital in Charlottesville. They're known for their trauma center. It's not that far from here."

Tom nodded. "Can you navigate?"

"Yes, next road, take a right."

The bleeding wouldn't stop. Her shirt was getting soaked. "Put more pressure on it," Tom said. *Christ, please don't die.*

"When Maxwell shot his gun, it surprised Blackfoot, and he cut me."

"Shit." Tom sped up.

"Slow down, Tom. Jeeps don't like mountain curves. Wait until we hit a highway."

At the hospital, Gail's side was covered with dark red blood, and the top of her jeans were soaked. He picked her up, and she winced. "Damn, that hurts."

"I'm sorry."

"Wait," she said, struggling to stay conscious, "we have to get our story straight."

"What, what the hell? I got to get you in there right now!"

"Listen to me, Tom, you were hiking on the trail and came across my cabin. I was packing up my Goodwill stuff. I asked you to help me." She winced, paused, and added, "Don't tell them anything about the Burno family. Do you understand?"

"OK." Tom was barely listening to her.

"Tom! Do you understand me?"

"Yeah, I got it."

"You mention them, and all bets are off. We're dead."

"I promise I won't mention them." Tom stumbled but caught himself.

Gail was out of breath but kept talking. "You were getting a ride from me. You wanted to take a break from the trail." Gail was speaking in short bursts, gasping between each sentence. "You were going to Charlottesville to look for some work. We saw a guy on the side of the road. His car had broken down. We stopped, but he fooled us, only a decoy, bait. He had blond hair, a young guy. He noticed my ring and tried to wrench it off my finger. I struggled. Told me to give it to him. I refused. He cut me and then took it, anyway." Her words drifted off.

"Gail, stay with me. Gail!"

She blinked hard, twice. Her eyes rolled back.

"You... understand me?"

"Yes."

"One other thing."

"What?"

"When we were stopped by the Bruno mafia, I put my ring in the ashtray. Take it, Tom."

"What?" Orderlies ran toward them.

"You take it!" Her face flinched, her lips pulled back, and her eyes tightened into little knots. "It can never be found, or it blows our story. And Tom, if the cops ask any questions, give them the simplest answers you can think of."

The orderlies slid Gail onto a gurney and rolled her away. A kind nurse nearby led him to the waiting room. A detective soon showed up. Said his name was Carl Nixon. He silently looked at Tom. *A man of few words?* He was a small man. His skin was sort of doughy, soft, you know. Even his voice was soft. Almost like a purr. Nixon asked what happened. Tom stuck to Gail's fabricated story; except he described her diamond ring.

"Did the robber have any physical markers that would set him apart?"

"Not that I saw."

"No tattoos, no scars, no jewelry, no strange clothing, nothing that drew your attention?"

"No, sir."

"How did he get away?"

"What?"

"How did he get away? You said his car had broken down."

This wasn't in Gail's story. *Simple Tom, simple.*

"The guy just took off. I guess the car wasn't really broken down."

"What kind of car?"

"I don't know, some beat-up jalopy."

Nixon wrote down everything. "So, he stabbed her, got the ring off her finger, and took off?"

"Yes."

"That's odd."

"Why's that, detective?"

"If she had a diamond ring, he would most likely assume there was more loot to be had. He would have searched the car. After all, you were in the middle of nowhere. What was the rush?"

Simple Tom, simple.

"Maybe because he had stabbed her, he got scared? Nixon nodded.

The detective was finishing up when a short, heavyset man with thick, horn-rimmed glasses knocked on the door and walked in like he owned the place.

"I'm sorry, sir; you can't come in here," Nixon said. Even with the intrusion, Nixon's voice remained calm.

The intruder straightened his gold-silk tie. He reeked of wealth, right down to his black crocodile-skin shoes and manicured nails. A big cop nearby told him that Detective Nixon was investigating the case.

"Detective, I'm her husband, Warren Roberson; what happened to my wife?"

"I can tell you that Mrs. Roberson was seriously injured and is being treated. Her status is unknown." He pointed to the waiting room. "Please sir, go have a seat in there. The nurses will keep you informed."

"No, I want to know how it happened."

Nixon shook his head. "I'm sorry, sir, but I am in the middle of an investigation. You need to wait out here until they know more."

Warren's lips twisted tightly.

"Sir, please sit down and try to be patient."

Warren left, snarling. He sat down but was too bent out of shape to sit there for long. He stood and walked back and forth in front of the window of the waiting room.

Nixon continued his interview. "I just don't understand it."

"What's that, detective?"

"Why didn't he at least take her purse? Or, if he was in a beat-up car, why didn't he take her Jeep?"

Remember, short and simple.

"I don't know, detective. What goes on in a criminal's mind? Maybe it was his first robbery, or maybe he knew we needed to get to the hospital. Who knows?"

"Maybe we'll get to the bottom of this." He nodded toward the waiting room.

"Stay close, Tom. There's a vending machine at the end of this hall, just to the left, if you want anything. "Oh, by the way, when the guy took the ring, were you in the Jeep or out of it?" Detective Nixon continued.

Tom thought through the story Gail gave. They stopped to help someone with a car problem. *Surely, she would say out of the car.* He half mumbled, "Out."

"So, he never touched the Jeep?"

"No. He never touched it."

Tom was escorted to the waiting room by the big cop. He found a newspaper, snuggled in a chair, and looked it over. Just to make sure he didn't hightail it, the cop stood next to the wall behind him. Tom could feel the cop's eyes glued to him.

Tom was reading the sports page when Warren appeared. "So, you were with my wife when she got stabbed?"

"Yes sir, I was."

"How did it happen?"

Tom told the story again. It rolled off his tongue.

"So, you just happened to run across the cabin?" His eyes squinted behind his thick lenses. "Just out there on the trail blowin' in the wind and you happened to come across my wife?"

"Mr. Roberson, I've been on the trail for months."

"And after you met my wife, you just happened to want to go to Charlottesville? And you just happened to stop and help someone on the roadside in the middle of nowhere? And you just happened to get robbed?"

Tom stood, towering over Warren. "What are you trying to say, Mr. Roberson?"

"I'm saying that I don't believe you happened on any of that bullshit story. What I am saying is that I believe you either did it or you were in on it. I am not sure which, but in either case, you got scared that she was going to die, is what I am saying."

Tom pushed his hand away. "You're crazy!"

"Yeah, how?"

Warren took a wild haymaker punch. He whiffed and fell to his knees. Tom lifted him from under his armpits. "Mr. Roberson, I know you're upset. I understand, but I'm telling you, you are all wrong about what happened." The officer broke them apart.

"Hey! This is a hospital. Go sit down. Another outburst and I'm going to have you thrown in jail."

Tom sat immediately. Straightening his tie, Warren asked, "What's your name, officer?" The officer tapped his badge.

"I just want you to know… I'm good friends with the chief of police, and I play golf with the mayor, so don't tell me what to do."

The cop moved close to Warren. "Go…sit…*down*."

More than an hour ticked by before a doctor wearing scrubs entered. He talked to the detective and then approached Warren. Tom listened in as best he could.

"It was a close call, Mr. Roberson. She lost a lot of blood, but she's stable." The doctor chose his words carefully. "We believe she's out of the woods for now. But we'll keep her under observation for the next forty-eight hours. After that, she'll still need a lot of rest."

"Thank you, doctor." Warren sighed heavily. "Whew, that was close. I want you to know, doc, I'm going to make a big donation to the hospital."

"Ahh, well," the doctor's brow furrowed, "that would be outstanding."

Tom shook his head. *The doctor saved his wife's life, and all Warren could do was offer money. Wow!*

The doctor walked purposefully away. The officer gripped Tom's shoulder like his hand was an industrial vise. "You're not to leave this hospital until the detective lets you go. You understand?"

"Yes, sir."

"Good." He released his iron grip. "Make yourself comfortable; it is going to be a long night."

Warren disappeared with a nurse. She was probably taking the jackass to Gail's room.

*

Tom nodded off in one of the most uncomfortable chairs on planet Earth. There was a shuffling of feet, soft bells ringing, and the sound of people whispering. *First the mafia and now this.* Callie came to mind. How she didn't wait for him. *I can't believe it. She's with my good old buddy, Jack... Yeah, go ahead Jack, make love to her, do all the things that I used to do.*

Tom had met Jack in college. They bumped into each other at a water fountain in the men's dorm. They were sophomores. Young and hungry for college experience. They immediately formed a bond. Jack was an outstanding athlete, and he turned the heads of the coeds. Hell, he had his way with the coeds. He was the guy every guy wanted to be. He had a sharp wit and an IQ that was off the charts. Deep down, Tom was jealous of Jack's talent. Why shouldn't Callie be infatuated with him...

"Mr. Hunt." Tom cracked one of his eyes. "Mr. Hunt."

Tom straightened up and raked his hand through his hair. Yawning, he said, "Good morning, detective."

"I talked to Mrs. Roberson." The detective handed Tom a cup of coffee. It was bitter but hot.

"How's she doing?"

"She slept well and is still stable." The detective was studying his little notepad. "She wants to see you." Tom nodded.

"Your story checked out. She confirmed everything you said." Again, Tom didn't say anything, he just gave a nod. *The less said, the better.*

"She verified everything, but I still have one nagging question."

Oh shit. "And what is that, detective?"

"She said that she was just getting out of the Jeep when she was stabbed."

"Yes?"

"You said earlier that the robber wasn't near the Jeep."

Tom's mind was racing. *Don't be wishy-washy Tom, stick to your story.* "No, you asked me if the guy ever touched the Jeep. He didn't. But I remember he was pretty close to it."

"*Hmm.*" The detective closed his notepad. "Well, everything checked out, so you're free to go."

"Thank you, sir."

"If you think of anything else, let me know. You take care, Tom." They shook hands.

*

Thank God Warren wasn't in Gail's room. He was such an ass.

Gail looked like she had aged ten years. Her face was puffy and tired; there were dark circles around her eyes and her hair was a mess. There were IV tubes in her arm. The nurse was taking her blood pressure. It was still very low from the loss of blood. The nurse jotted down a few notes on Gail's chart and left.

"How are you feeling?" Tom asked.

"Like a bulldozer ran over me."

He held her hand. "Thank you for everything, Gail."

"Did you get the ring?"

"Not yet. I'll get it when I get my pack."

"Good." She gave a strained smile. "I've talked to Warren about helping you get a job."

"Wow, I think you've done enough; besides, he thinks I was the robber."

"He realizes now that you saved my life. You got me here just in time." She was exhausted.

"Maybe I should let you rest." He gave her hand a soft squeeze. "I'll come back tomorrow."

"No Tom, Warren is a very suspicious man." She tried to give a little laugh, but it turned into another wince. "He might realize I've got an attraction for you."

"I should get back to the trail."

"The harshest month of winter is on us, and that can be brutal in the mountains, Tom."

"I know."

She closed her eyes but kept talking. "I've got a deal for ya."

"A deal?"

"Yes, I asked Warren for a favor." Gail still had her eyes closed, but she was trying to shift a little in the bed. It was a costly move. Pain. "We own a country western bar named Miss Kitty's."

"I'm listening." Tom helped her shift over.

"Hand me that call button, please," she said, indicating that she wasn't going to wait any longer for more pain medicine.

"Anyway, you can bar tend there until the weather gets better." She pressed the button multiple times.

Tom thought about Pat. He was supposed to meet Pat in a few days, but as they always said to each other, "If it doesn't work out, nice knowing ya." *Good luck, Pat, I hope I see ya around the bend.*

"That sounds good, Gail. Do you know any cheap places to rent?"

"Yes, I know a great one. There's an office and a bedroom above the bar. It has everything you need: a fridge, stove, shower, and a bed. We let workers stay there from time to time until they get on their feet."

"Are you sure Warren is good with this? He tried to fight me earlier."

"You did him a favor, now he'll do you one. Trust me, you probably won't see him again. He never goes to Miss Kitty's anymore."

"How much a month for the apartment?"

"Don't be ridiculous, Tom. There is no rent. We like helping people."

An older nurse came walking into the room and interrupted. She helped Gail lean up to take some pills. "You've got about ten minutes before she's asleep."

"What did you give her?" Tom asked.

"A new drug just out on the market called oxycodone." She checked Gail's temperature. "I'll be back in about an hour to check on you, sweetie."

"How's the Oxy working for you?"

Smiling, she said, "Pretty damn good. When they kick in, I feel no pain… So, what do you say to our offer?"

Tom nodded even though Gail's eyes were still closed. "Sounds like a deal I can't refuse."

"It's done then. You can go there now," Gail slurred, "just go to Miss Kitty's and talk to Kojack. He knows you're coming."

Chapter Ten
Charlottesville, Virginia
1974
Light Up My Life

The music was blaring. People danced to a sweet song called "Dance with Me (Just One More Time)" by Johnny Rodriguez. Next up, a fast-paced two-step that worked well with "Sunday Mornin' Coming Down" by Johnny Cash. Miss Kitty's was a popular country western bar by any standards. Plenty of dance rooms and lots of action. Guys hit on girls and girls hit on guys, and they all drank too much.

Tom worked at the bar from six p.m. until two a.m. Tuesday–Saturday. Behind the bar was nice and safe. Unlike the bouncers, he didn't worry about getting a fist in his face trying to calm down some pretend cowboy, or for that matter, cowgirl.

On Thursday through Saturday, Miss Kitty's had live entertainment, and the place was frequently packed. Tom knew most of the regulars by name. As soon as he saw one before they even approached, he began pouring their preferred drink. Most of the patrons were good tippers, so the money was good. And, on occasion, a young lady waited for him and visited his accommodation. Tom was flat-out having a blast.

Everything in the bar was moving smoothly this particular Friday night. Kojack, the manager, worked the weekend nights behind the bar. He was a middle-aged football jock that played tight end for the Virginia Cavaliers football team in the early 60s. His claim to fame was that the Cavaliers tied the NCAA record for the most games lost in a row, twenty-eight.

Tom poured a double Jack and Coke; just a splash, said the man. He looked at least three sheets to the wind already.

"Hey, Tom," Kojack called out.

"Yeah?"

"Guess who just walked in?"

Tom shrugged. "I've no idea."

"Jane."

"Jane who?"

"The boss's daughter. She's finishing up college this year."

"Ohhh, that Jane. I'd like to meet her."

"She's cool." Kojack pushed a couple of beers across the bar to two cowboys. He rubbed his swollen, knotted hands. A bad case of arthritis caused by football. "Man, she's not just cool, she's fine."

"So, you've got a crush on her?"

"Hell yes. If I wasn't the manager here, and if I wasn't already married, and if I wasn't an old fart, I'd be chasing her."

"OK, I can understand the marriage restriction. Age gap, maybe. But I'd never let work stand in my way."

"Going after the boss's daughter is very risky, pal. You know what they say, if the boss doesn't think you are good enough for his little girl, you're fired. If the boss's daughter drops your ass, you're fired..."

"Yeah, yeah, I've heard all that before. If you bring her home late, you're fired. If she cries because of you, you're fired. If you get her drunk, you're fired. Blah, blah, blah."

"Word to the wise, Tom, don't be a dumbass."

"Yeah, I hear ya." Tom flashed a mischievous grin.

A young blonde wearing a white crochet cap, white shirt, red coat, and bell-bottom blue jeans slid silkily into one of the bar stools. "Hello, Kojack."

"Jane! Wow, it's been ages since you've been here. Heard you're graduating this year."

She gave a big thumbs up. Kojack's tone changed. "How's your mom?"

"She's doing better. Rehab helps a lot."

Jane searched her purse for a cigarette. Before she could find her lighter, Tom held a lit match. She looked up and gave him a warm, welcoming smile. *Hmm, same smile as your mother.* If Jane and Gail were the same age, they would look like twins. Same eyes, same lips, and same delicate jawline... Jane leaned toward the match. "Thanks." She even had the same low, breathy voice.

"Jane," Kojack patted Tom, "this is Tom Hunt."

"Nice to meet you, Jane."

Her photo at the cabin had been taken years ago; she was far more grown up and even more beautiful now.

Jane gently blew out a relaxed stream of light grayish smoke. "I know who you are, Tom. My mother told me all about you."

"Oh? Hope it was good stuff."

"You're the guy walking the trail. You were with her when she got robbed. I owe you a big thank you for saving her life."

"No, the doctors saved her life. I just got her there in time."

"Well, I like a man who doesn't boast. Let's just say, if you weren't there, my mother probably wouldn't be here now."

Tom gave a single nod. "You care for a drink?" Others were waving for another round. Tom ignored them.

"Do you know how to make a Harvey Wallbanger?"

Tom silently poured vodka, Galliano, and orange juice and gave it a good shake. "Here ya go, one superb cold Harvey Wallbanger." Tom waited.

"*Hmm*, not bad, Tom. Not bad at all."

"Tom!" Kojack yelled. "We need more Bud."

"Jane, I'll be right back."

"I'll be here, cowboy."

Kojack worked his way over to Jane. "So, Jane, what do you think of the new guy?"

"He's a lot cuter than Mom described. She said he was a half-starved, lost soul with depressing eyes."

"And how would you describe him?"

"Good looking. Smart and witty. The total package."

"All of that from a one-minute introduction?"

"No, I figured that out by the time he lit my cigarette."

Kojack laughed. "Be careful Jane, that boy will be gone soon."

Jane flipped her ashes into a smoker's sand bucket/ashtray. "Spoken like the brother I never had."

Tom hauled two cases of Bud to the bar cooler. They were armed and ready for the next big wave of Bud drinkers, always a rowdy bunch.

Jane held up her drink to Kojack and smiled. "Besides, he makes a damn good Harvey Wallbanger."

Chapter Eleven
Charlottesville, Virginia
1974
Tangled Web

Time flew by. Days turned into weeks. And Tom was getting antsy. The worst of winter had passed, and the mountains were calling him. He knew this day would come. But once again, he had a choice. Before he had the choice of adventure or Callie. Adventure won, and he lost Callie. Now, it was the same equation, except this time, it was Jane.

Tom was taking it slow with Jane. It had nothing to do with her being the daughter of the boss. Nada. He knew what was really holding him back. It was Gail. How could he tell Jane that he went to bed with her mother? But how could he keep it a secret if they go all in? He couldn't live with the lie. Talk about a lose/lose situation.

They were, by now, set in a daily routine. Breakfast. Workout. Miss Kitty's. They ate a late breakfast every day at a mom-and-pop restaurant called Lil Peggy's Biscuits. Today's special consisted of Virginia country ham, red-eye gravy, eggs, homemade biscuits, and of course, stone-ground grits. Talk about delicious. The restaurant was originally a brick grocery store built in 1946. The old brick and heavy wooden floors gave it more than a certain charm. It was a classic. The decor was simple: a set of long tables with six chairs per table, plastic table covers, and family-style dining. Waitresses constantly brought in fresh platters of food. If you were not a local, you would never even stop here.

Tom got a second serving of eggs and biscuits and another slice of that heavenly Virginia ham. Jane started her after-meal cigarette ritual. Tom watched as she inhaled deeply. It looked so satisfying, the way she smoked it.

"My dad's a cardiologist in Atlanta," Tom said helpfully.

"I was wondering when you would tell me about your family."

Tom motioned for a refill. "He was one of the early guys that said smoking was bad for you. He even made me promise to never smoke."

"Did you promise?"

"Yep."

"Tom, I've seen you smoke reefer."

"Hey, he only made me promise not to smoke cigarettes; he didn't say anything about other things."

"Ah, a loophole."

"Anyway, I was just wondering. Have you ever thought about stopping?"

She theatrically ground her cigarette into a nearby ashtray. Tom couldn't tell if he pissed her off or if she was symbolically showing she hated cigarettes.

"I'll stop smoking today if you'll tell me one thing."

Tom sat up straight. "What's that?"

"Are you interested in me, or not?"

"What? Hell yes, of course. I'm interested in you."

She reached across the table and put her hand on his. "Then why haven't you even made a move? Do you just want to be friends or something?"

"No, of course not. I want to be more than friends. It's just that…"

"Just what, Tom?"

"I'm leaving soon, Jane. Next week, I get back on the trail."

"I'm sorry Tom, but I have to call bullshit on that."

Jesus, I knew this day would come. Gail would never forgive me, and neither would you, Jane, if you knew the truth.

Jane continued, "I know you gotta finish the trail. But we can have this moment now. If you choose to come back this way, maybe I'll still be here for you." Jane was still holding Tom's hand. She squeezed it tightly. "You know the saying, *be here now*."

"Yeah, but I don't want to hurt you."

She pulled her hand away. "That's BS, Tom. You're not worried about hurting me. You're the one that has the wall up. You're the one that doesn't want to get hurt."

Silence. Tom broke the ice. "Let's get out of here."

She cut her eyes and sighed wearily.

*

Tom needed a good workout, so they went to the Y. Tom treasured his time working out. Minimal chitchat. Treadmill, weights, and a little one-on-one. Jane was a well-rounded athlete. She had played basketball in high school. So, she enjoyed shooting hoops with Tom. She was pretty impressive at Twenty-one, not to mention beating him at horse too.

After the workout, Tom felt pretty damn good. His head had quit spinning around. Back at Miss Kitty's, they went up to his little apartment. He put on an Eagles album, *Desperado*, and pulled out a couple of cold PBRs.

"Here ya go."

"Thanks."

The first word she had spoken to him since breakfast. She had given him the silent treatment during their workout.

How do I get out of this freakin' hole I've dug?

"Listen, I'm going to take a quick shower and get ready for work."

"Is that an invitation?" she pressed.

Shit… it's now or lose her. Tom nodded.

There may be nothing sexier than taking a hot, steamy shower together. Nothing. They held on tightly, moving in small circles. Hot water pummeled them. They didn't talk, but they certainly did laugh a lot. Pressing against each other was insanely exciting. They quickly toweled off – sort of – and then they raced to the bed.

*

Miss Kitty's was kickin' for a Thursday. The band was known around Virginia, so they expected lots of fans to come from all around. They played some Waylon and some Oak Ridge Boys, Willie, and Kenny. A half-witted cowboy asked Jane for a dance. She liked to dance; besides, Tom was stuck behind the bar. Which was not all bad because he sucked at dancing. No rhythm in his body or his soul. There were only a few couples dancing.

He was a tall guy with a bad case of wandering hand syndrome. The guy eased his hand down from her mid-back to her lower back to the top of her ass. She broke away when he started fondling her there. She slapped him. Hard. He was shocked. Left standing in the middle of the dance floor looking like a jerk.

"Want me to throw the asshole out?" It was Kojack.

"No, it was just cheap thrills. Let it go."

"Jane, how about a drink?" Kojack asked.

"Thanks, but I've lost the mood. Maybe I should go back to that guy and grab his ass."

Kojack winced. "I'd rather you not."

"Listen Kojack, do me a favor."

"Sure, anything."

"Tell Tom I'll wait for him upstairs."

"Sure. I'll tell him."

Tom was happy to finally close up and call it a night. He was worn out and ready to sit back, relax with a cold PBR, and listen to a little Stones. He unlocked his door. A cold feeling prickled down his spine. Something was wrong.

"Hello, Jane?"

"In the kitchen, Tom," she said hesitantly.

Tom's gut twisted. Something was wrong. Jane was sitting at the kitchen table, drink in hand. She held it up. "It's not as good as yours, but it'll do in a squeeze," she slurred.

"How many have you had?"

"Not enough."

"What's wrong, Jane?"

"Oh... I don't know. Why don't you tell me, Tom?"

"What are you talking about?"

Jane took a large sip of her drink. She spilled it down her shirt. She wiped her mouth. "You know," she said, pointing her finger, "my mom always told me that when someone is trying to hide something, you need to call bullshit at least three times to get to the truth." She wagged her finger. "Bad boy. Because I love you, I don't push you for the truth."

"What are—"

"Don't play dumb, for God's sake." She swept her drink right off the table, smashing it onto the floor. She slammed her hand on the table and looked hard at Tom. Jane pulled her mother's diamond ring out and slammed it on the table.

Oh shit. "Jane, you've been going through my stuff?" Tom blanched.

"Yep. Guilty."

"You were in on the robbery, weren't you, Tom?"

"It's not what you think."

"Oh really, despite what my eyes see?"

"Jane, you gotta trust me. I didn't rob your mother."

"Bullshit." Jane walked past Tom. She opened the door. "Goodbye, Tom."

She was halfway out when Tom yelled, "Your mother gave it to me." Jane stopped dead.

"Jane, come back. Let's talk this through."

"I want it all, Tom."

Tom told her the entire story from the moment that he ran into the Burno family to his near OD on drugs to his revenge in Waynesboro to getting help from her mother. The only part of the story Tom left out was that he had slept with Gail. Was it because he wanted to protect her from knowing that her mother had an affair, or was it because he was too scared to tell her?

She asked a dozen questions and then sat in thought about what Tom had told her. "I promised your mother I would never tell anyone about the Burno family because if the word got out, they would come after us."

"And you're saying my mother and father do business with the Burno family and that's why you got away without being killed. Because my mom asked for a favor."

"Yes."

"Wow." She retrieved the icy vodka. "Here, have a drink." He enjoyed a nice swig.

"Tom, you're holding back on me."

"That's all I can tell you."

"Bullshit! Tom, what are you not telling me?"

"Don't make me tell you."

"I won't make you, Tom, but if you don't, I'll call it quits." Jane poured another shot. "This is our moment of truth."

Oh, God. Jane waited silently.

"If I tell you, then you'll walk out. If I don't tell you, you'll walk out." Tom poured another shot.

Jane bit her lower lip. "Jesus Christ, you just told me." She dropped her head into her hands. "What's the only thing that could possibly make me leave you… oh shit, oh no." She looked up. Tears rolled down her cheek. "You bastard. You slept with her, didn't you, Tom?"

Chapter Twelve
Charlottesville, Virginia
1974
Once is Nothing, Twice is a Habit

Tom tossed and turned all night. Miserable from his fight with Jane. To top things off, he had a serious panicky nightmare, waking up several times, groaning and sweating. He was running naked down a mountain trail. His feet were torn, bleeding, and bruised. The wind howled and blew wildly. It was difficult to keep his balance. A lightning bolt obliterated a small pine a stone's throw away. A pack of wild, starving, gray wolves cornered him at the top, growling, showing their yellow razor-sharp teeth. Rain pelted down, stinging his skin. Lightning exploded again, not fifty feet away. He was stuck on a mountain cliff with a slashing river at the bottom. He had a choice, but no choice. Be ripped apart by the wolves or jump. The wolves stealthily moved forward, with rumbling growls and hungry mouths. They got so close that he could smell their collective breath, an overpowering stench of death. The closest wolf leaped in an instant, grabbing the back of his calf, and ripping out muscle and tendon. Blood splattered on the frenzied wolf's muzzle. He backed away, meat dangling down. Pain. Such intense pain! He jumped and hit the water feet first. The water was icy! He gasped. The slashing current grabbed and twisted him violently. He gasped for air, but the river was relentless. Tom fought for his life.

He was going down, sucked into the fluid vortex. He couldn't escape. Something strong grabbed him and, with one quick jerk, slung him on the bank. He found himself looking up into the good Samaritan's eyes. Oh, yes, yes, yes, yes! It was his beloved trail buddy, Pat.

Bam! Bam! Bam! "Tom, open this damn door!" Gail shouted. Tom shook his head. *Wow, what a dream.*

Bam! Bam! "You better open this door right now." In worn-out jeans and his favorite Grateful Dead t-shirt, he greeted her. Or maybe it wasn't a greeting. It was an ambush.

"Are you fuckin' kidding me, Tom? You told my daughter that we slept together? Are you crazy?" Gail stepped into the room, flushed with anger. Her lips were trembling. She unleashed a mist of saliva. "You broke the rules, Tom. How dare you! After everything I did for you!"

"Gail, I didn't tell her. She figured it out."

"There're hundreds of girls in this town, and the one girl you go after is my daughter. She's the most precious relationship in my life and you're trying to destroy it!"

"It wasn't like that, Gail."

"Do you realize the damage you've done?"

"I didn't mean for this to happen. She found the ring and thought, I robbed you. Jane thought I put you in the hospital."

"Better that than telling her that we fucked!" Gail screamed.

Tom threw his hands in the air. "As I said, I didn't tell her. She put two and two together."

Gail crossed her arms. "OK, I am listening."

Tom told her exactly what he had said to Jane. "She knew I was holding something back on her. She called bullshit and wanted to know the whole truth. I told her I couldn't tell her because if I did, she would leave me. That's when the light bulb went off in her head."

"And you didn't deny it?"

"Didn't confirm it either. She drew her own conclusion."

Gail's eyes squinted tightly. Her nostrils flared. Tom was completely at a loss for words.

"I've got to meet Warren in a few minutes, and we need a plan."

She was wearing a blue midi dress, high heels, and nice gold jewelry. A sign she was heading to a socialite event. Good news for Tom; she would be out of his face soon.

"You don't have a choice. Tell the truth. If you dodge it or try to deny it, she'll never forgive you." Tom sat down wearily and rested his elbows on his knees. "She'll never respect you, Gail, unless she knows you've told Warren."

Gail looked up at the ceiling, arms still crossed. Tears rolled down her face. Big fat tears. "This is worse than being stabbed."

"I'm sorry. Sooner you tell Warren, the better."

"What, why?"

"Because you'll be able to tell Jane that… either you and Warren are on the same page and that you guys are going to fight for your marriage, or you and Warren are getting a divorce."

She stared at the floor. "He's going to be pissed, but he has no room to talk."

"What? He's had an affair?"

"Affairs, plural. He hires young assistants that are eager to get promoted."

"Does he know you know?"

Gail rolled her eyes. "I told him as long as they stay in the back seat, I don't care. To tell you the truth, I'm glad he has girlfriends. That way, he doesn't want anything from me."

"How long has this been going on?"

"We haven't had sex for years."

"So, it's been years since you've had sex?"

"I didn't say that. I said no sex with Warren in years. Regardless of what happens, Tom, you need to leave, and I mean now! Get back on the trail, damn it, and don't show your face around here again."

*

Tom turned in his keys to Kojack at high noon. They shook hands and said their goodbyes. *Pretty dramatic, huh?* He was the only person Tom was going to miss. He never connected to his other coworkers. Kojack gave him a present. One of the bar's merch items was a silver flask with the name Miss Kitty's written on it. Appropriately, it was filled up with a delicious bourbon, Southern Comfort.

Snow was still falling before the start of spring. Tom hoped he wasn't soft and out of shape. Thumbing was always fun. It was a people-meeting adventure.

A two-door maroon Buick Riviera pulled up. Three young black men with no smiles.

"Need a ride?"

"Where're you heading?" Tom asked.

"New York City," a deep voice replied.

Hmmm, New York? The Big Apple?

"Don't have all day." The big man pushed.

Tom nodded. "Sounds cool to me."

Two minutes later, Tom was sitting in the black seat as the car spun off.

"My name is Earl, but they call me Duke."

"Duke? How'd you get Duke for a nickname?"

"You've heard of Duke Ellington?"

"Jazz player?"

"That's him. I love jazz so much they nicknamed me after him." Duke's deep, rolling, soft laugh was beautiful. "I think he should've been named the king, but I guess because he was black, he could only be a duke."

Laughter exploded from Tom. "I don't know much about music, but it's a pleasure to meet you, Duke."

"Over here," pointing at the driver, "is Billy. And the dude sitting next to you is my good man, Booker. If you haven't noticed, they're identical twins. They do everything together. They're both musical whiz kids, very quiet dudes, and they don't like to socialize."

They were mirror images. "What kind of instruments?"

"They don't like to brag. Three, or is it four, Billy?"

Billy kept his eyes on the road and just shrugged.

"Oh, for God's sake, Booker, how many?"

"Four."

"Let's see," Duke kept count on his raised hand, "trumpet, saxophone, trombone…and…"

"Clarinet," Booker answered.

"Wow, can't imagine!"

Duke continued, "Man, if they're apart, they get some kind of weird anxiety and I know they read each other's mind. It's some kind of identical twin shit."

"That's crazy." Tom studied them. "So, you guys play in a band?"

"Yeah, the rest of the band is already there. They set things up," Duke explained.

"What's the name?"

"Duke Jazzbo and the Kool Kats."

"Take it you sing and play the…"

"Piano. Sing sometimes, but we've got a gal named Patti… and man, she has a killer voice." Duke rubbed his hefty chin. "Why are you hitchin' around?"

"I've been on the trail."

"Man, that's some crazy shit." Booker looked like he smelled something bad.

Billy nodded. "Leave it to a white boy to think tramping around the mountains is cool."

Duke pulled out a joint. "Want to smoke a doobie? Or are you not really hip?"

"Absolutely."

The smoke made a soft, thick gray cloud in the closed-in space. Billy slapped in an 8-track.

"Wow, that's some good shit, man," Tom said.

"Talkin' about the joint or the music?"

"Both."

"You like reggae?" Booker asked.

"I like this guy. Tom was already bogarting the joint. He took another killer hit. He started coughing so badly he could not hold it in, not even for a second. "What's his name?"

"Man, were you born in a fucking barn? Never heard of Bob Marley?"

Tom shook his head. The others laughed. They laughed so hard and long that they forgot why they were laughing. It was a reefer laugh. Tom joined in, too. A red light flashed. The laughing stopped. Instantly. A cop car was flashing its lights. Thank God it wasn't too close on their bumper.

"Holy shit," Duke tossed his weed out the window. "We need air!"

"Taking my sweet time, brother." Billy rolled into a side street.

"Everybody be cool…"

The cop strolled up to the car, putting his hat on and looking stern. "Well, well, well. What do we have here? Looks like Mary Jane is paying you a visit. Considering the sweet billowing smoke."

"Oh, no sir," Duke said. "That's incense smoke."

"What in tarnation is incense?"

"Incense." Duke opened the glove box.

"Stop!" The cop pulled his gun. He was obviously well practiced.

Duke froze. Hands in midair. "Sorry, officer, I was going to show you a stick."

"No need. What's it for?"

"It drives away negativity and smells so sweet."

"What the heck?"

"Officer, please let me explain," Tom asked.

"Get out of the car, son. Why are you with these boys?"

"Just hitchin'."

"That's pot I smell, isn't it?"

Is this some kind of test? "Yes."

"And what did you do with it?"

"Threw it out the window when we saw your lights."

The cop looked back.

"You're going down to the station, son."

"Sir, um," Tom sighed, "Officer?"

"Roberson."

"Did you say Roberson?"

"That's my name."

"You know Warren and Gail Roberson over in Charlottesville?"

The cop put his hands on his hips. "You know them?"

"Oh, yes, sir. I helped Gail when she got robbed."

"I heard all about that robbery. Warren's my cousin. Tell these boys you saved their asses."

*

"What the hell just happened, Tom?" Duke's jaw dropped as the cop spun away.

"Know his cousin."

The others started laughing good-naturedly.

"Man, you're fuckin' with me?" Booker scratched his head.

"I knew it would pay off to pick up this whitey." Duke laughed.

Billy peeled off in a billowing cloud of blue smoke. Marley's sweet, beautiful music flowed out of the speakers.

Next stop, New York, New York.

Chapter Thirteen
New York City
1974
Different Strokes for Different Folks

Rush hour in the big city. Inching along. A clusterfuck of cars slammed up. Honk! Honk!

"That SOB flipped the bird at me!" Booker screamed.

"Welcome to New York," Billy said.

"Tom, where you stayin'?" Duke asked.

"Don't have a clue."

"Tom, this ain't no town to go floppin' around. You planning to crawl down some alley to sleep?"

"And what, cover myself with boxes?"

"Hang with us. We're playing at Lenox Lounge in Harlem."

"Yeah, man, you should watch our gig," Billy confirmed.

Wow, Billy wants me to come. "Booker, your thoughts?"

"Don't take this personally."

"I won't."

"You may know the mountains, but this is Harlem. There's a lot of shit out there. New York's finest do not play around."

"Hey, I was born in Atlanta."

Duke laughed. "Run in the hood a lot, did ya, boy? Diggin' with those whores, druggies, gangs, and pimps? Cops behind the drug lords. Get in their way or even look at them wrong. Those dudes will send you to the garbage heap." Tom was silent.

"That's what I thought, Tom. Grew up with money? Have you been shot? Stabbed?" Still silent.

"Blade at your throat? Straight razor? Shaken down?"

No, but I've been forcefully fed drugs and later nearly killed by drug runners. "I get the point. I had a cushy life. That's why I'm here now."

"Cushy? That ain't the word for it, Tom. Face it, you've been pampered. You're clueless out here."

Yep, he did grow up in the elite Buckhead section of Atlanta, Georgia. The CEO of Coca-Cola lived down the street. No, he had never been in a gunfight or a knife fight. Never been robbed. A speeding ticket, overturned by a judge, was the extent of his cop harassment.

"So," Duke said, "it's settled. You'll hang with the band."

*

The Lenox Lounge was empty. It was a small bar with heavy jazz vibes. Photos of jazz heroes lined the walls, Gottlieb, Jordan, Davis, all of them. It was dark. It was smoky. Just like a jazz bar is supposed to be…

Sound check. Duke was the main attraction, but the singer, Patti Cruz, stood out. Even warming up, her voice was so velvety, smooth, and tight. Cheerful, breezy, and lively. Tom was blown away.

Tom guessed Patti was in her mid-twenties. Long black hair, high cheekbones, and one of those delicate swan-type necks. She was wearing a beautiful stage dress and a classy, sparkly evening gown. When she was singing, she was in seventh heaven.

After their sound check, Tom met her at dinner. The bar treated the band. Tom included. Burgers, fries, and a bunch of drinks. Tom had a Miller.

"Where you from?" *Wow, Tom, that line should dazzle her, you playboy you...*

"Costa Rica, you?"

"Atlanta." Tom finished his burger and ordered a Jack and Coke.

"Like it sweet, do ya? Corn syrup, whiskey, sugar water. Delightful."

Tom took a gentle sip. "It's sweet all right."

"Ugh."

"Got something better?"

"Yeah, try Jameson. An Irish whiskey with a little soda water or just plain water."

Tom ordered two drinks: one Jameson with soda and one with plain water.

"Can't let you taste test alone." She ordered the same.

"Sorry, I'm late Patti."

Tom looked over his shoulder and saw a woman in her early thirties, chocolate skin, soft hair, a round face, large almond-shaped eyes, and a small mouth. She was wearing a white halter top and tight bell-bottom jeans. In the dark club, her halter top was a prominent attraction.

Patti got a big hug. And a big kiss.

"Hello, babe."

"Sweetie, sorry I'm late. Traffic sucked."

"Tom, meet Connie."

"I'm so excited you finally made it home." Their embrace was more than friendly. "It's been ages since you've come back. Your tours are brutal."

"Taste test time; you in?" Patti smiled.

"Hell yes, baby."

Well, something is going on here. They were very close friends or gay. A fifty-fifty shot.

First up, Jameson and plain water. Tom grinned. "Pretty good."

"No hangover like you get with that sugar crap you drink," Patti claimed.

Who is this lady and what does she mean to Patti?

They tasted Jameson and soda.

"Nope, not this one." Tom wiped his lips and pushed his drink away. The ladies laughed.

"It's our favorite," Patti said.

The band settled onstage. Duke tested the mic and then started playing "I Got It Bad and That Ain't Good", by his idol Duke Ellington.

"I need to get on set; the two of you should get to know each other," Patti instructed.

"Break a leg, baby."

After a few songs, Connie asked, "What do you think, Tom?"

"Of?"

"Their music, of course."

"Love it. Thought they were going to be a straight jazz band, but this stuff is great."

"Yeah, it's the new jazz sound. They infuse Latin and African jazz. You heard of Carlos Santana, or Chick Corea?"

"Heard of Santana, but didn't know how to categorize his music."

"Well, Tom, if you are going to hang with my girl, you better get on top of her music."

"My girl?"

"What's that?"

"You said, my girl."

Connie got close to Tom. "When Patti's here, she's mine."

"What about when she's not here?"

"I don't ask. What she does when she ain't with me is up to her."

"Interesting relationship, Connie."

The band was finishing their set. Tom clapped loudly. Their first set was killer!

Chapter Fourteen
New York City
1974
Sweet Dreams

Break time. They exit to the back alley. Booker lit one up. Passed it around. Tom took a sweet hit. The stench of old garbage ruled the alley. Not even the sweet aroma of good weed helped. There were large brown rats. Nasty. Big as wharf rats. Half buried in rotten cabbage, lettuce, potatoes, and other scraps.

"My dad told me those things were alley cats." Duke laughed.

"What?" Tom asked.

"Yeah, I was ten before I realized we lived in a rat-infested slum."

"Bastards have sharp-ass teeth," Booker inserted. "Got bit once. Felt like a darning needle going through my finger."

"Messing around with a rat?" Tom asked.

"Yeah. Did it all the time. They would get on top of our trash bin. You grab 'em by the base of their tail and whip it real fast. It breaks their back."

"Did it get away?"

"Yeah. Guess I didn't swing hard enough. Never tried that shit again."

"So, what's the deal with Patti and Connie?" Tom asked.

Duke took a solid hit off the joint. Smoke curled brazenly out of his mouth. "Patti's what you call a free spirit. There's only one Patti."

"Connie her girlfriend?"

"That bitch doesn't own, control, or even influence Patti. She's holding on for dear life, and to be honest, she's held on longer than I ever thought she could. Patti's story is like a lot of downtrodden people, Tom. You're going to think what I tell you is cruel and unimaginable."

"I'm listening."

"Patti's cousin raped her when she was eight. The bastard was eighteen. It wasn't a one-time deal. Her daddy played pool with the guy at the local bar."

"He find out?"

"Hell, he knew. Blamed her."

"No way."

"Yes, way. Her dad beat her with a belt for enticing her cousin. You can still see nasty welts on the back of her thighs."

"Wow, can't imagine."

"Gets worse. Father married her off to that cousin prick of hers when she was sixteen. Patti pleaded not to. Pleaded. Pleaded. And pleaded…"

"She run off?"

"Sure, Daddy found her and brought her back."

"So, she married him?"

"Oh yeah, they got married. One night, the SOB came in drunk and stoned and raped her again. She slammed one of those big, black, heavy cop flashlights right into his temple. Apparently, she kept it next to her bed to fend him off when he came home like that."

"Jesus, did it kill him?"

"Hell yes."

"Then what happened?"

"Judge tried her in youth court. Called it a heat of passion murder. Forgot what degree charge that is, but it doesn't matter because the jury said it was self-defense."

"Sounds awful. That's why she stays away from men?" Duke nodded.

"How did she wind up with the band?" Duke checked his watch.

"Heard her sing in the streets one night. Singing a cappella. Had a bucket full of cash. Knew then she was special. And the rest, as they say, is history." Duke walked on the stage and Patti followed to nice applause.

Once again, Patti mesmerized them for the rest of the evening. Their final set brought the house down. "Little Sunflower", "Send in the Clowns", and "Red Clay". They played "Fever" for their encore. Peggy Lee would have been snapping her fingers to this hip cat version.

*

The bar closed. The band celebrated. Duke pulled Tom to the side. "Patti said you should stay over at Connie's with them. It's the best option. Besides, they say I snore louder than a buffalo."

"With severe sinus problems," Booker added.

"Gee, I wonder what I should choose?" Tom joked.

Connie's little one-room apartment was crazy small. The living room was pale blue and fitted with a modest dark blue couch. Tom's soon-to-be bed. A small coffee table had an old, cool radio on it. The kitchen was the same. Both rooms had that 1930s Art déco style.

"That's the whole show, Tom. I'll get you some blankets and a pillow." Patti said.

"OK, if I turn on the radio?"

"Sure, knock yourself out."

"Let It Be" by the Beatles popped up. Patti walked in wearing a T-shirt and bikini underwear. "Here's your pillow and blanket." *Holy shit!* She put his bedding on the couch and casually walked back to her bedroom. "Good night, Tom."

Chapter Fifteen
New York City
1974
It's Nature's Way

Night after night, the denizens of the Lenox Lounge partied hard with the band. Die-hard lovers of jazz music. But all things come to an end. And tonight was it? Time to pack up. Tomorrow, the band hits the road. Charleston, South Carolina. No rest for the weary.

The trail was calling Tom. The Green Mountains of Vermont were legendary. The White Mountains of New Hampshire were equally touted. The Presidential Traverse was the toughest the trail had to offer. A perfect test.

The music began cranking up. Connie joined Tom.

"Tom, let me buy you a drink."

"No."

"No?"

"Let me buy you a drink."

"Have to admit, Tom, didn't like the idea of you staying at my place, but Patti said she thought you were cool. And to my surprise, she was right. I've enjoyed meeting you, Tom, and I wish you the best."

"Thanks to you, I got some sleep. I heard Duke has a loud-ass snore."

"When do you take off?"

"One more night at your place, if you're cool with that?"

"Of course, Tom."

"Leave tomorrow after breakfast."

The band had been a huge success. A successful gig indeed. At three a.m., they started packing up.

"Shame you don't blow a horn, Tom," Duke said.

"I wish."

Duke wiped his brow. He loosened his tie.

"Man, you're a good luck piece. Got the cop off our ass. Now, we've made more money on this gig than any on our tour."

"Been a real blast, man."

Duke pulled out a small chain with a quarter-sized coin on it. "Want to give you this, Tom. It's my Saint Christopher. The patron saint of travelers."

"That's nice, but don't you need the protection more than me?"

Duke put his massive hand on Tom's shoulder. "Have two of them. My father passed away and I got his. He wore it through WWII until the day he died. So, I want to give you mine. Served me well over the years."

"Thanks, Duke, I'll wear it always."

Tom slipped it down his shirt. *A ring, a flask, and now a Saint Christopher.* Each with a story to tell.

"Didn't know you were religious." Tom grinned.

"You kidding me? Our music is the essence of spirituality." Tom shook Duke's hand.

*

The moaning in the bedroom said Connie and Patti were home. Endless sexual desire. He closed his eyes but was unable to ignore the laughing and giggling. They were really going at it this time. Finally, he was almost asleep. Now the moaning sounds were softer and right beside him next to his bed. It was Patti, wearing nothing but beads of sweat.

"Tom?"

"Yes?"

"Want to join us?"

*

Patti's hand stirred Tom in the morning. Patti and her big brown eyes.

"Good morning,"

"Thought you didn't like men?"

"Don't, but that doesn't mean I don't want them."

"Same with Connie?"

"Not so much."

"Now you tell me. The day I'm leaving."

"It's meant to be, Tom. I'm afraid of getting attached. It always gets messy for me."

"Always?"

"Yes, always."

"Messy for you and Connie."

"Will be. I'm not staying here anymore. Next time I'm in New York, I'm stayin' in a hotel."

Connie was still out cold.

"How do you think she'll take the news?"

"Don't care."

"That's cold."

"I believe in ripping off the bandage. Zap. Tell them point-blank: Sorry baby, found someone else. Been great knowing ya. Wish you the best. Then get the hell out of Dodge and don't answer the phone."

One minute you are an item, the next, poof, you're history. Just like Callie and Jane. Poof.

"What's the reason?"

"She wants to go on the road with me. No way!" Connie stirred.

"I'll clear out before the fireworks?"

"Don't blame you."

Tom quietly gathered his things. "Take care, Patti."

"You too, Tom."

*

Greenwich Village was historical. The 50s Beat Generation and the 60s hippies. The village was electrified with energy. Artists, writers, and musicians overflowed the sidewalks. Bohemian hippie dresses, long hair and beards, tie-dyed T-shirts, blue jeans, and sandals. Peace, love, Mother Earth, and spirituality. Defiance of materialism and authority.

A sudden windy rainstorm came in, raindrops splattered wildly on the cement. A small herbal store looked inviting and cool. The Indian flute music was so calming. Crystals, healing rocks, essential oils, and jars of herbs lined the room. Astrology, yoga, mysticism, and all sorts of esoteric magazines. A short lady in her mid-fifties was dancing gayly around the store. Her shag was stylish with bangs. Peculiarly, a golden-yellow patch covered her left eye. Waving a smoking bundle, she circled the room clockwise. She stopped in front of Tom and stared directly into his eyes. "May I help you remove your negative vibes?"

"What?"

"The negative vibes. Your aura is clouded with negativity."

"OK… ah… I guess so."

She moved the smoke all around his body.

"Lift one foot at a time; I have to get your feet."

"What is this stuff?"

"Sage. It's cleansing and healing. American Natives have used it in rituals for ages."

She was wearing a maxi tie-dye dress, a crystal necklace, and colorful boho earrings.

"Name's Sally."

"Hello Sally, I'm Tom. What were you saying about my aura?"

"Your aura is cloudy. Your heart charka is clogged."

"What can you do?"

"My table's back here. Come on."

"Think that's exactly what I need. Why not?"

She led him to the backroom where a massage table dominated the room. He settled down and relaxed. She moved her hands slowly down Tom's body.

"It's what I thought. Your heart chakra has stagnated." She placed an amethyst crystal on his forehead.

"This will enhance your intuition and calm your mind." She placed a rose quartz crystal directly on his heart.

"Have you lost someone recently?"

"No one has died."

"No, not death. A relationship? Someone you are closely connected with?"

"Yes. Several."

"The love was deep?"

"Yes. One was named Callie and the other Jane."

"Did they find someone else?"

Tom rubbed his shoulder. Clearly uncomfortable.

"Sally, my best friend ended up stealing Callie."

"And you haven't forgiven her or him, have you?"

"I don't think about it. It's over."

"And the other one?"

"Jane… well, Jane threw me out for a good reason."

"Let's focus on Callie for now. Keep your eyes closed and think about her."

"This rose quartz will help you forgive and build your self-esteem."

"My self-esteem?"

"Yeah, you think that your best friend and girlfriend did something to you? It feels to me like you didn't think you were worthy."

"What?"

"Is your father a powerful man?"

Tom's eyes popped open. "Yes."

"Can never live up to his expectations, can you? You need to realize your own unique potential in this world."

Sounds like hippie talk.

"Get yourself centered, Tom."

"Centered?"

"Yes, know yourself. Trust your abilities."

"And is that why I lost Callie?"

"Yeah, you sabotaged your relationship. Blamed your best friend for backstabbing you. But it was you that caused all the drama. It came from the inner voice of your father. You proved you're not worthy."

OK, enough psychobabble. Tom took off the healing rocks and sat up.

"Christ, come on, Sally."

"Am I wrong?"

"Probably not, but…"

Sally removed her eye patch. Beneath it was a beautiful sky-blue glass eye. A symbol was on it. "I was born with only one eye. Do you like my Turkish Nasar? It keeps evil away and fuels my psychic intuition."

"You're a spiritual medium?"

"Yes… I'm a healing guide. I help people find their spiritual and emotional well-being. Now, let's get back to your chakras. So, what happened to the other girl, Jane?"

"No, I've had enough for one day."

Her glass eye never blinked. Probably for the best. "You should think hard about what has been said. It came through me, not by me."

Tom laid down. Sally placed the healing rocks and crystals back in place.

Hope the rain passes soon.

Chapter Sixteen
New York City
1974
Destiny

Swirling wind and heavy rain sat atop the city. The temperature was dropping. A simple turn of an old wooden door sign and the shop was closed.

"Best plan on staying here tonight, Tom. You can use the backroom table as a bed."

"We've never met, and you'll let me stay?"

"Told you, I'm psychic. You've got a good aura."

A gust of rain beat against the windowpane. Thunder rumbled repeatedly. "Given the conditions, I believe I'll accept your offer... Got any chores I can help with?"

Sally pointed to several cases of inventory. Spiritual books, healing rocks, incense, and herbs "Can you stock those for me?"

"Sure. By the way, how are you going to deal with this crazy-ass rain?"

"Not a problem. I live upstairs. A nice, cozy little apartment."

Just like Miss Kitty's.

"Awesome." Wind rattled the windows again. "It's pounding now."

"Yeah, a regular derecho storm."

The lights blinked. Stayed on. Blinked more. And then shut off.

"Damn it, not again."

Tom looked out the window. "Streetlights are out. The whole block is out!"

"Swear, there're more storms these days. They seem harsher, too."

"Had my fair share of nasty storms on the trail."

"Read an article in Time magazine about the weather. Said the global climate is getting cooler each year and that at some point, there will be another ice age."

"Guess I like cold better than hot."

Lights flickered again. Boom!

"Holy moly, was that a transformer? No electricity tonight. Good thing we have a little more daylight."

She pulled out a couple of lanterns and gave Tom a flashlight. Tom started stocking the merchandise. The first book he picked was called *The Doors of Perception*. It looked strangely intriguing.

"Sally, have you read this?" He held up the book to show her.

She smiled broadly. "Written in 1954 by Aldous Huxley, and it's a classic."

Tom read a random sentence. "The urge to transcend self-conscious selfhood is, as I have said, a principal appetite of the soul."

"*Hmm*... So, this is why you hike."

"What?"

"Tom, you're on a metaphysical quest?"

"No, not really. Just testing myself."

"Take it, Tom. And come with me this weekend. I am going to visit a close friend. His name is Cabot."

"Where does he live?"

"You're going to like this. He lives in the mountains of Vermont, right off the trail."

"What?"

"Lives in what's called the Bennington Triangle."

"Like the Bermuda Triangle?"

"Yeah. Strange stuff has happened there. You know, UFOs, bigfoot, and strange sounds and lights scaring the bejesus out of people. The Algonquin believed it was haunted… There was a malevolent stone. Step on it, be devoured."

"Talk about a coincidence. I was heading to Vermont."

"What do you mean, coincidence?"

"I mean, it just happened. I had nothing to do with it. Like a pinball machine, the ball happens to fall one way or the other."

"Wait, didn't you choose to come into my store?"

"Only because of the rain."

"Didn't you choose to come to Greenwich Village?"

"Well, yes but—"

"Tom, either every moment of life is a coincidence, or the choices you make create your destiny."

"Destiny is just good or bad luck."

"Totally disagree with you, Tom. Destiny is in your control."

"What?"

"What you face in the future is a result of the choices you make today. Who you are is the cumulation of all your choices."

With that, Sally went upstairs.

*

First thing Sunday morning, they took off. Sally's yellow VW hippie van had a psychedelic wizard surrounded by surrealistic flowers and peace signs painted on one side. A multicolored unicorn on the other. Nice ride for Sally.

It was going to take some time in this old van. Seven hours without stops. Bob Dylan, Jimi Hendrix, George Harrison, and Joan Baez sang and played all the way there. Tom's bizarre trail experiences kept her mesmerized. Some of them were really dicey.

"Tom, this adventure, as you call it, is really your metaphysical awakening."

"I don't know, Sally. Everything that happens is not connected to destiny."

"No. I don't think so, either."

Tom nodded, very pleased that she agreed with him.

"I know they have a connection."

"Why?"

"You look, but you don't see. You hear, but you don't listen."

This girl has been on one too many acid trips.

"OK, spell it out."

"The departure of your fraternity brothers. Simple. No one else can walk this path with you."

"Is this like dream analysis or something?"

"The mafia group was a sign of evil. You must confront evil. And you did. Your vision revealed that when you were a boy, you were deeply steeped in the metaphysical world. Your parents represented the cultural norms. You were seen as strange. But in fact, your imaginary friend was a great sign. And a bigger sign was that you saw an angel. And that, Tom, is a rare gift."

Maybe she's tripping now.

"Go on."

"Gail and Jane... You're so selfish. You didn't care about them. You know, Tom, when, or if, you grow old, you'll remember everything you did badly to others, and unfortunately, you'll barely remember the good things. It's nature's payback."

"So, you believe nature has a conscience and knows everything I do?"

"Tom, you're part of nature."

"OK, well, what about Kojack?"

"Kojack may seem like a minor connection, but he was there to show you that no matter where you go, you'll have friends. Not everyone has that capability. It's one of your great talents. You'll never be without friends."

"OK, fast forward to Duke."

"Duke was a good and powerful lesson. You're not listening to your intuition. When you first met him, you saw a car full of blacks. You ignored your intuition. If you'd listened to it, you'd have seen a big, gentle soul. The good news is your intuition kicked in after you got into the car."

"That leads us to Patti and Connie."

"So many good lessons. Your world has been very structured. Everything has its place. You're conditioned to follow rules."

"I'm a rule follower? My parents wouldn't agree with that one."

"Because they are very strict rule followers. You've been taught to paint within the lines. But the reality is scribbling outside the lines. Patti was a curveball." She paused. "Which side did you experience that night? Your feminine or masculine?"

"What?"

"I'm going to take a guess. She was on top. Her masculine side was in full gear. Did you let go, Tom? Did you feel your feminine side that night?" Tom looked out the window and said nothing.

"Everybody's a mixture of yin and yang. It's okay to express both sides. You'll never feel the full power of your sexuality until you do."

"You're saying, I'm part woman?"

"No… I know you are."

"OK, Sally, have to think about that one."

"On some metaphysical trip, you'll see your other side."

"I'll seriously be interested if that happens."

Traffic was slowing way down. Two cars were slammed together. There were police cars and ambulances everywhere. A body bag was disappearing into the back of an ambulance.

"You forgot Pat."

"Left Pat last on purpose. He may be your biggest connection to the metaphysical world."

"Pat?"

"He showed up out of nowhere, right?"

"Yes."

"He never went to town?"

"No."

"Never starving?"

"No."

"Never lost weight and never flinched at the weather?"

"True and true."

"Interesting."

"So, what are your thoughts?"

"I'm just guessing, but maybe a spiritual guide. I'm sure you'll see him again, Tom. When you least expect it, he'll be there." Sally picked up speed and jacked up the radio.

Chapter Seventeen
Outside of Bennington, Vermont
1974
The Whole Is Greater Than the Sum of Its Parts

Sally turned down a gravel road. Too late to hike up to Cabot's log cabin. Staying in the van was the best option. Her van was made for camping. It was essentially a bedroom on wheels, with plush dark-yellow shag carpet on the floor, walls, and ceiling, coupled with a nice mattress, blankets, and pillows.

She stopped next to a small creek. It was flat with plenty of trees.

"Never seen a van as cool as this one."

"Only thing I hate about shag carpet is I keep losing my roaches in it."

Sally giggled as she pulled out a joint. She took a monster hit.

"Damn, that's good. That drive was a bitch."

"You need help with that?"

She grinned and passed it over to Tom.

"If you'll make a fire, I'll heat up some food."

"Deal. Whatcha got?"

"A mixture. Brown rice, broccoli, carrots, seaweed, some cashews, and a little something extra special."

"Sounds hearty." Tom hid his smirk.

A dead sugar maple tree was perfect for collecting firewood. They're known for a few sparks and less smoke.

A beautiful crisp night with a sliver of moon and stars abreast.

"This stuff is awfully chewy. Taste like dirt."

Things just naturally got kind of quiet. His solar plexus tingled. The dark sky had a lightly colored spiraling dust trail. Stars were exploding everywhere. It was Van Gogh's *Starry Night*.

"Did you lace the weed?"

"No, I put some magic mushrooms in the rice."

"Holy shit."

Tom's mind was racing. He was freaked out. He struggled to breathe.

"Take it easy and let go, Tom. I promise you'll enjoy it. At this point, either go along or be dragged."

"Why did you do that?"

"You need shaking, Tom. Let go of your ego. Remember what Huxley said? Walk through the doors of perception."

"Stay with me."

"I'm with you. Seeing trails?"

"Oh, yeah."

"Like colorful shooting stars."

"Yeah, I do. Wow."

Everything was strange. Words sounded strange. His voice was not his voice.

*

"The sky is crazy wild with colors. It's like an abstract painting. Except it's moving!"

"That's energy! Crazy, huh? Tripping is called tripping for a reason. See my aura yet?"

"Sally, you're all bright yellow and gold.

"That's my chi energy."

"Your what?"

"Its spiritual vibration. See anything else?"

"You're one wise woman…"

"Good. You've noticed that everything around me is either yellow or gold."

Suddenly, Tom was in front of a big metal door. The same as before. Pennies lay all over the ground. They all had the same year, 1898.

"Now I'm looking at a big clock. Stopped at… 12:12. When those crazy-ass hillbillies shot me up with LSD, it was 11:11!"

"Well, that was then, and this is now. As it always is… Angels are comforting you."

He was unable to speak. Unable to move. Trance like.

A gate opened slowly. Loud screeching sounds. A brilliant light shone. It illuminated the same path he had followed before. He walked to the end. No childhood home this time. The most beautiful woman he had ever seen stood staring into his eyes.

Their energy entwined. Tighter and tighter.

Sally talked without talking.

"Tom, this is your twin flame. She's your yin mirror; she's the other half of your soul."

"I've seen her before."

"Where?"

"My dreams."

"Erotic?"

"Very."

"Wasn't sex you experienced? It was the fireworks of your souls connecting together."

Her flame was fading.

"She's leaving now. Don't go!"

"Tom, don't fight it!"

"Please stay. No, don't leave me!"

"Let go!"

A flash of glittering bright green. She vanished.

"Will I see her again?"

"Yes."

"Will I meet her in this life?"

"Probably not. You have the same karmic issues that must be worked out. When you do that, you'll meet her. Together, you'll ascend to the fourth dimension."

"How can I make that happen?"

"With your life path number."

"What the…?"

"Yours is the number seven. Means you're a thinker. Very spiritual and analytical. A truth seeker. You'll need all your mystic powers, intuition, and spiritual awareness. She is waiting for you at home."

"OK… Her name?"

"She doesn't have a name. She's a vibration. You're the same. Like a musical note."

*

The morning sun peeked into the van. Tom had no idea how he got there. *Damn, I'm naked.* Sally was naked.

"How did you sleep, Tom?"

"Slept great. Jesus, how did I get here… like this?"

"What's the last thing you remember?"

"My beautiful twin flame disappeared."

"OK. You came out of your trance fast. Rocking back and forth. Speaking gibberish. We lost our telepathic connection."

"Go on."

"Well, you stood up and took your clothes off. You started telling me that I was the most beautiful woman you'd ever seen. You begged me… if you know what I mean?"

Tom listened with a stoic face. He didn't remember anything. *We had sex?*

Sally laughed. "Had ya going, didn't I? Sometimes I crack myself up. You would've gone through the rest of your life believing you jumped in the sack with an old, overweight bag of bones with one eye." Tom bellowed. "To be honest, Tom, your aura isn't developed enough for me. Yeah, you've got a nice body, but your spirit... Let's just say I would have turned you down. You ain't what I am looking for, kid."

"So, what did happen?"

"Like I was saying, you just crashed right out of your vision. You were rocking all around. You stood up. You fell down."

"You mean I tripped?"

"Yeah, right into that freezing creek. Help me, help me. I came over to try and help, but you pulled me right in. Asshole." None of it was on his radar. "I helped you take your clothes off and crawl into the van. We crashed hard."

"Coming off a vision always that abrupt? Bam back into reality?"

"No, it's a sign that you were learning too fast. Maybe learning more than you were ready for."

"Just have one question."

"Shoot."

"When we talked about Patti and Connie earlier, you told me I would experience my feminine side."

"Yes, I remember."

"You did that to set up my vision, didn't you?"

Sally smiled. "Of course not, Tom. That was just another one of your *coincidences*."

Chapter Eighteen
Cabot's Log Cabin, Vermont
1974
A Different Path

A steep, winding trail led them to Cabot's log cabin. The trail was tedious and uninviting. Every switchback, Sally wanted a break. For the last five years, Cabot had been living in his cabin in the middle of nowhere. To get basic supplies meant a hike to his neighbor. A kind old man who let Cabot use one of his barns to store his 1958 Chevy pickup. The nearest store was miles away.

"Couldn't imagine hiking this with a lot of heavy supplies," Sally said.

"Would be a challenge all right."

"Least it's still summer. Easiest time of the year to do this crazy trek. It's also Cabot's favorite season."

"He gardens?"

"Oh, yeah... he has a great garden."

Summer was a time of stockpiling. Cabot had a dirt cellar. A nice twenty-eight to forty degrees year-round. He was a born hunter. Instead of a gun, he favored his crossbow. Though guns gave him an unfair advantage. Deer, snowshoe, cotton-tailed rabbits, grouse, and lots of turkeys. He smoked them all. He also smoked fish, carp, freshwater drum, and bowfin. His chicken coop had plenty of eggs and chickens to eat. He grew plenty of vegetables in the short Vermont gardening season. He canned peas, green beans, tomatoes, squash, and cucumber.

Sally told Tom all about Cabot's background. He had a degree in electrical engineering. Served in Vietnam. His unit was a badass long-range reconnaissance patrol. He experienced death. Lots of death and the smell that goes with it. His life expectancy as a radio operator was less than thirty seconds in battle. A fifty-pound radio was part of his standard equipment. Made him slow and clumsy. The dense jungle foliage made it necessary to have an extended ten-foot antenna instead of the standard three-footer. It acted as a flag for enemy shooters. Then there was the noise. The damn noise. The volume dial was on the back. By the time you could get to it, your enemy had a beat on you.

"Showed me a photo of his unit once. They wore black pajamas and non-la hats. Made them look like the Viet Cong. Confused the bastards long enough so our guys could shoot them."

Sally was sweating profusely. Tom was sucking air himself.

"Whatever you do, don't bring up the war."

"Yeah, I've got friends who went to Nam. Never the same."

"Cabot wasn't the same either. The horror of war was etched into his soul forever. Nightmares of heads stuck on spears. Heads lining a wall with their genitals stuck in their mouths. Fear is what they were after. And it worked."

"He told you all of that?"

Sally nodded. "You have any questions? We'll be there soon."

"Nah. I'm good."

There was a small cabin. It was a one-room tin roof structure with a fieldstone chimney. The foundation was strong. Logs notched at the ends, with a mud pebble chinking. Cabot sat in a sculptured stump chair. It was a lustrous northern red oak. He had several of them placed around the table.

"Hello, Cabot." Sally took her pack off. "That climb up here is not getting any easier."

"I wondered who was stomping around my mountain." Cabot focused his sharp green eyes on Tom, but continued to talk to Sally. "Suppose you came up for the festival?"

"Of course, it's the biggest event of the year."

"Can always use your help, Sally. Who's the traveling compadre?"

"Tom Hunt. He'll stay up here for the festival if that's okay with you?"

What festival? Sally, you didn't say anything about the festival.

Cabot stuck out his hand. "Tom, any friend of Sally's is good by me. Welcome to Wolf Moon Rising."

"How did it get its name?"

"It's the name of this mountain," Sally explained. "Native Americans had vision quests here on the first full moon of the year."

"You can hear the wolves howl like crazy in January," Cabot added.

"Every January, I come back and join Cabot and a few others for a ritual quest."

"That's the only two times I ever see this gal, the festival and the quest."

"Don't want to crowd ya, Cabot."

Cabot had a beard down to his collarbone. Scars on his face and neck. Gashes on his hand. One across his nose. One on the side of his neck. Several slashes on his right hand. *Perhaps he got it tangled in some barbwire.* His hair was in a ponytail like an aging hippie. Maybe it was the harsh winters, or maybe it was Nam. Something made Cabot weathered and hard.

Tom admired the chairs and table.

"You make these?"

Cabot half laughed. "Everything you see, I made."

"Wow. They're incredible. What did you put on them?"

"Linseed oil followed by a special wax. How about you? You make furniture?"

"No. But I'd love to learn."

"That can be arranged. Working on a couple of new pieces now."

The one-room layout of the cabin was very spacious. A stacked-rock fireplace. Nice furniture, but not much.

This dude is a minimalist. The kitchen was small, but it had a stove and there were lights in the ceiling.

"Got electricity up here?" Tom asked.

"I put in a 5kW hydroelectric system with a Pelton wheel design that runs off that stream a few hundred yards from here. Has a strong waterfall that's perfect."

"There goes the electrical engineer in him." Sally rolled her eyes. "You might as well bark at us, Cabot. We have no idea what you are talking about. Talk English."

"Well, it works great for a small log cabin, except the turbine gets clogged up from time to time. It's a bitch when that happens in the dead of winter. But, hey, at least that stream is big enough and flows hard enough that it never freezes in the winter."

"Pelton wheel design? Sally's right… Greek to me." Tom had a blank look on his face.

"Old technology. Invented back in 1870. Extremely efficient."

"As I said, Greek to me."

"Give it up Cabot." Sally laughed.

There was a closet with a curtain in front of it.

"You have a shower?"

"No." Cabot opened the curtain on a square wooden handmade tub.

"Man, that's beautiful," Tom said.

"Wait till you get in it." Sally rubbed the wood surface. "I love this thing."

"Cabot, you get hot water?" Tom asked.

"It's a wood-fired hot tub."

"How long does it take to heat up?"

"Not long at all in the summer," Cabot winced, "but in the winter, it sometimes takes an hour."

"I bet; you spend a lot of time chopping wood?"

"It's not so bad. I'll show you my homemade log splitter."

"Got to say, you're one self-sufficient guy."

"You want some herbal tea? I was just about to make some goldenrod and ginger tea."

Tom nodded. "Sally tells me you know a lot about herbs."

"Medicinal herbs and mushrooms. There's a ton of raspberry leaf, St. John's wort, yarrow, red clover, goldenrod, basswood, and burdock root around here. As far as mushrooms go, I find chaga, reishi, and maitake. I sell my stuff to a holistic health food store in Middlebury."

"And he finds the best magical shrooms in the country," Sally added. Cabot ignored Sally.

"I've packed a bunch of products to take down to the store tomorrow if you would like to tag along?"

"Don't fall for it, Tom. He's wanting you to carry a pack of supplies up here as well." Sally sat down in a chiseled stump chair in front of the fireplace. "The pack won't be heavy going down. Coming back is a different story. Right, Cabot?"

"I do have to get more supplies."

"Tom, your pack will feel like a bag of cannon balls coming back up the mountain," Sally added.

The teapot was whistling. Cabot poured three cups.

"Not bad," said Tom. "I also like the golden color. What does it do?"

"Muscle relaxer and anti-inflammatory."

"I'd like to learn more about herbs."

"Hang here for a while and you'll learn."

They sat and enjoyed their tea.

Chapter Nineteen
Cabot's Log Cabin, Vermont
1974
Gypsy Spirit

"Appreciate you coming along, Tom."

They had packs full of herbs and mushrooms. *No magic shrooms.* Hiking down the mountain was a skip and a jump. A half mile from the bottom of the mountain was an old barn. Cabot's truck was parked in it.

"So, Cabot, this beauty is your famous Chevy?"

"Yeah, let's hope it starts."

Dark gray smoke puffed out of the tailpipe when it finally started. Sounded like a spoon stuck in a blender.

"Listen to that engine purr." Cabot patted the dash.

"Yeah, real smooth all right."

"After a while, the grinding sound will quit, haha."

They meandered down the road. Very slowly.

Hope this thing can go faster than thirty. Or is he just that laid-back?

"Cabot, how did you meet Sally?"

"We lived in the same commune."

"You guys lived in a commune?"

"Thought I would give it a try."

"What was it like?"

Cabot stroked his beard as he reflected.

"At first, it was cool. But after a while, it wasn't."

"Something specific?"

"Yeah, not everybody works hard."

"People took advantage of you?"

"Oh, yeah…everyone gets an equal share at the end of the day. So, it pisses you off over time. You start resenting people."

"Can love 'em, but can't live with them?"

"More like you want to slap them upside the head," Cabot replied.

"I get the picture."

"Sally got disillusioned, too. So, we both split."

Cabot changed gears. The spoon in the blender sound was back.

"Have to say, never met anyone like Sally," Tom said as he grinned.

"Nope, only one Sally."

"Think she has psychic powers?"

"Yes, no doubt she's clairvoyant. And her power of precognition is amazing. She avoids negative people, so she must be receiving good energy from you."

Cabot picked up speed. *Well, I'll be… the truck can go forty.* Then it started rattling again. He dropped the speed back to thirty.

"She never told me about any festival."

"Once a year, people come up for a good time."

"A mini-Woodstock?"

"Very, very, mini."

"Good bands?"

"Just locals."

"How big is it?"

"Around three hundred showed up last year."

"That's very cool, Cabot."

"That's why I want to build a stage and a few outhouses. It's getting bigger every year."

"Assume you need help?"

"All I can get."

Cabot pointed to a sign. Middlebury: 4 miles.

"We have the festival over in a meadow near the stream. People bring tents and chill out for a long weekend. Hippies and gypsies, and the occasional cool lawyer. A lot of music... lovin'... skinny dippin'... and pot smokin'."

When they arrived, Cabot popped open his truck door, smiling; it sounded like the hinges needed a good squirt of WD-40.

The old country store was a converted barn painted dark red with a thick, planked wood floor. As soon as Tom walked into the store, he saw a beautiful young woman mixing herbs. Long skylights ran across the ceiling. The soft, diffused sunlight captured the woman's face very nicely. Artificial light makes people's skin, teeth, and eyes look dull and sickly.

The natural light brought out how healthy, high-spirited, and radiant she was. She smiled at him. Her eyes reflected the light beautifully. One eye was silver tinted, the other was multi-colored with silver and a drop of amber. No makeup on her face. Her long, straight, sleek black hair was a silky curtain all the way below her waist. Her chipped-tooth smile made her so cute. And it made Tom so happy. Her faded old blue jeans coveralls were a perfect touch. Tom would not have been surprised to see a straw sticking out of her mouth. A small, gold-leaf pendant accented her long, beautiful neck.

"Tom!" Cabot called out.

"I'm over here." He was looking at some homemade soap a few aisles away.

"Tom, want you to meet Tara?"

Tom scooted away from the soap to meet her. "I'm Tom Hunt."

"Welcome to Nature's Magic, Tom. My name is Tara Miller."

"She's our master herbalist… Best in the state."

"That's a beautiful pendant," Tom said.

Tara grinned. "Thank you, it's a Bodhi leaf."

"Is it symbolic?"

"Yes. That's why I wear it. It reminds me to follow the tenets of my religion."

"What does it mean?"

"For Buddhists, the Bodhi leaf symbolizes spiritual awakening and wisdom."

"You're a Buddhist?"

"No, not officially."

Tom thought her voice sounded playful and soothing. A water fountain was in the corner of the room. He was thirsty. But he couldn't keep his eyes off Tara.

"Unofficially?"

She laughed. *Damn, her laughter was infectious.*

"I like studying the Buddha. Cabot introduced me to Buddhism."

"Cabot?"

"Cabot is very protective of letting people know the real Cabot."

"The real Cabot?"

"Yes, hopefully he lets you in."

Note to self: read more about Buddha, and ask Cabot about it.

Cabot interrupted. "Tara, I got a lot of jewelweeds this time."

"Great! Time for more of my special salve."

"Salve out of an herb?" Tom asked.

"It's not hard. You decoct the stem, remove the concentrated liquid, and mix it with some good old beeswax and aloe vera, and voila! Magic cure for poison ivy!"

Tara concocted a dandelion tea to drink while they continued to chat. Their packs full of supplies were much heavier than herbs. Cabot favored large cans of food. Things like seventy-two servings of whole egg powder. Thirty-two servings of Egg noodles. Forty servings of freeze-dried sliced strawberries. Five-pound bag of all-purpose flower.

"Hope to see you at the festival, friend," Tom said as they left the store.

Cabot laughed. "Oh, you'll see her there all right. She's the main singer. Plays guitar and sings like an angel. Her group can jam!"

"Their name?"

"Why, Nature's Magic, of course."

*

It was a beautiful sunrise. A few colorful clouds hung lightly in the sky. Tom inhaled deeply. The mountain air. Nothing is like the mountain air.

Something moved. It was Cabot in the nude doing yoga. *Amazing!* Each graceful move flowed into another pose. *Later, revealed to be the Scorpion yoga posture.* He was dancing. He moved into a graceful handstand.

Jesus, that takes incredible strength and flexibility.

Cabot finished in a full lotus pose. Tom was about to stand and applaud when Sally came around the corner. She had been watching Cabot as well. She too, was naked. She came up behind Cabot nestled her face into his neck and began breathing with him in rhythm. Breathing in harmony. Her hand eased down over his heart and slowly made small circular motions. She slowly moved down and stopped on his belly button. She let her hand drift lower and stopped at different spots on Cabot's body, repeating her measured number of circles. Tom wanted to get closer but was petrified of being seen. Sally moved in front of him and sat down on his lap. Their rhythmic breathing got louder and louder until Sally's head rolled back. She gazed into the sky, moaning.

Holy Jesus.

Tom was aroused. The intense moaning stopped. Cabot and Sally were sweating, locked in a hug. Sally rose, kissed Cabot on the head, and walked away.

*

Grassy flowered field. Large rocky stream. Mountain ridges rolling for miles. A sloping meadow. The stage.

Cabot had stacked peeled pine logs. His plan was simple. Make four big frames and attach them to the legs. The frame was standing sturdy by the end of the afternoon. The flooring was next. Banging nails all morning long sure was tiresome. Cabot wiped his brow.

"Tom, we're going to need more nails."

"Do they have nails at Nature's Magic?"

Cabot smiled.

"What?" Tom asked innocently.

"You just want to see Tara again?"

"Well, if she's around, I'd say hello."

"Don't give me any of that BS, Tom. As soon as you laid eyes on her, you lit up like a firefly. Hormones don't lie."

"Hey, you're one to talk. I saw you and Sally this morning. Nailed together tighter than the wood on this stage!"

"I know you saw us."

"You knew?"

"Of course. Sally wanted you to watch."

"What?"

"Sally is all about teaching lessons."

"What lesson?"

"Sex is critical for spiritual development. But not like you know it."

"Cabot… you guys knew."

"Your presence was felt." Cabot pointed to the stream. "Let's take a dip."

"It didn't bother you?"

"What did you see?"

"You did yoga first, then you started meditating… I'd like to learn yoga and meditation."

"Pay attention."

"OK. Ya'll were breathing exactly together."

"Yes, our auras were joined."

"She was rubbing over your heart."

"Yes, to unleash my love and compassion."

"She rubbed in several places."

"Each was with purpose."

Going from a casual walk, chatting, to a choppy trot. Soon they were racing to shed their clothes. They stopped at the edge of the stream and then jumped in. Sweet. Cool. Water. Actually, cold water. Very cold water… The ubiquitous mosquitoes dive-bombed their exposed heads. *The bastards are the size of freakin' hummingbirds.*

Cabot said, "Continue, Tom."

"She circled you and sat down. Assume you were in her?"

"You assume wrong."

"You had orgasms?"

"Absolutely. Multiple."

"All right, then, I want to know more about this stuff."

Tom dunked his head. He popped up and slung his hair back.

"Hey, let me use your clunker." Tom winked at Cabot, and Cabot laughed. "I'll go into town."

"OK, tell Tara hello for me."

Chapter Twenty
Cabot's Wolf Moon Rising Mountain Festival, Vermont
1974
Why Take One When You Can Take Two

People everywhere. Tie-dye tents everywhere. A veritable human ant hill. No plans. Grab a spot and claim it.

A white flag with a red cross marked the medical tent. Cabot's physician friend was ready for just about anything. Injuries to ODs. There were also dehydration tents all around.

From above, the festival grounds were marked with multicolored poles. The meadow was so large that they acted as a compass. A psychedelic, face-painted child squealed and ran away from the yelping dogs. The whole festival was shimmering with freedom. Bam! Drum roll! "Ready! One, two, three…" It was the Jefferson Airplane's "Don't You Want Somebody to Love."

"Hey, Tom."

"Hey, Sally! That's some kind of beautiful tie-dye hippie dress! Shake it, baby!"

"Dance with me! Yeah, woo-ha."

They jumped up and down, throwing their arms all around. "Best of My Love" by the Eagles blasted out. At the end of the song, they collapsed to the ground.

"So, what do you think of this place?" Sally asked out of breath.

"I love it up here!"

"Yeah, may stay up here myself."

"What, you and Cabot getting together?"

"Oh, hell no. He's a hermit. I'd drive him crazy."

"OK, so why?"

"Because I'm going to… Tom, I'm going to lose my store."

"What? Why?"

Sighing heavily, she shook her fist at the sky. "Errrrr… the bank."

"The bank? What about the bank?"

"My damn loan."

"Yeah."

"Interest keeps rising. And the vendors. Oh my God, do I owe vendors money? A ton of money. And fuckin' credit cards. Face it, I'm broke."

"Sally, you know how you're always talking about destiny?"

"Yeah, fine, destiny I created."

"I'm starting to understand it now."

"What about it?"

"Give me a second."

Tom scrambled into his tent. The third song blared out. Joe Cocker's "A Little Help from My Friends."

Everybody swayed and sang. Tom emerged all smiles. He handed her a small box. "Sally, this has a lot of negative karma. But I think that is about to change."

Sally opened the box. Her jaw dropped. "Tom, is this ring real?"

"Oh yes, very. Remember the story of Gail and her daughter?"

"Yes."

"She didn't ever want to see it again. Told me to get rid of it."

"Tom, I can't take this. It's worth a fortune."

"Sally, I'm doing what Gail asked me to do. I'm getting rid of it. This way, it can do some good."

Sally hugged Tom. "Jesus, this will clear all my loans and then some."

"As a wise woman once said... your path led you to this."

"Thank you, Tom." A tear trickled down her cheek. "Better put this in my van. By the way, I'm reading palms and tarot cards. Come by later."

"Groovy."

"See, you'll be a hippie yet."

"What does that mean, anyway?"

"It means Helper in Promoting Peaceful Individual Existence. Stay trippy, little hippie!"

*

The band was on break. Twilight was fading. The half-moon glowed.

"Hey, stranger." It was Tara standing behind Tom.

"Tara, I've been looking for you." He gave her a big hug.

"Well, you found me."

"Wow, you look amazing!" She wore a braided leather hairband with several peacock feathers attached to the strap. *Very cool.*

"Figured if I hung around the stage long enough, you would show up."

"Where are you staying?" Tara waved her hand across the sea of partyers.

OK, so every time I get around Tara, my throat gets a lump in it and my mouth dries up.

"The pole that's red in the sunlight. Hard to see now. Where did you pitch yours?"

"Don't have one."

"Staying in the cabin?"

"No."

"Tara, I'm totally confused."

"Figured I would ask a friend to share his tent."

"Ohhh, a friend?"

"OK, a new friend that happens to be tall like you and has a beard like you and…"

"Think I know that guy."

"So, what will he say?"

"He's a damn fool if he doesn't say yes."

"Are you always this complicated, Tom?"

"Don't know, do ya?"

"Thought you were a simple man."

"Maybe. You'll have to hang with me longer to find out." Tom glowed with pride. He ran his hand along the edge of the stage. Solid. This mountain, this place screamed home.

"Tom... Tom, come up here." Cabot stood with a group of confidently composed men at the back of the stage. "Guys, this is Tom Hunt."

In rapid fire, he blurted out the name of each man. "I want to thank you guys for volunteering."

Volunteering? To do what?

"Whoa, what are you getting us into?"

"Crowd control."

"What?"

"Fights. So many fights. I'm prepared this time."

Damn, Tara is why I'm here.

"You want me to play bouncer?"

"Yeah. You and Jason will make a great combo. I'll be sitting back here if you need me."

A kid for Christ's sake... Peach fuzz, blond curly hair, and he's a string bean. Hardly instills fear. Probably sixteen.

"Where're we stationed?" Tom asked.

"Red pole area."

"Cool, see you over there in a few minutes. Need to talk to Cabot..." Tom pulled Cabot aside.

"Cabot, you kidding me? He's a baby kitten!"

"That kitten you're talking about is a second-degree black belt."

"Damn!"

"Been teaching him since he was in grammar school. Fighting to him is like hiking to you. Trust me, that kitten can turn into one hell of a badass. So, if the shit hits the fan, let him do the fighting and you come to get me."

*

Tara's band, Nature's Magic, took the stage and erupted with Jefferson Airplane's "White Rabbit." Tara was the perfect Grace Slick.

The sticky sweet smell of pot wafted seductively through the undulating crowd.

The first drunk badass stumbled up. The dude was pissed. Swinging around an empty bottle of Wild Turkey. A foul, drooling loudmouth. Hitting on a little hippie girl. She did not want to be hit on.

"Leave her alone, pal," Jason stated icily.

Tom was right behind Jason. The guy tried to sucker punch Jason. He barely flinched. The so-called badass stumbled and fell.

"Going to ask you again. Just one more time… leave her alone."

"Fock you!"

A bull charge. Wham! Jason slammed him to the ground and twisted his wrist hard. Screams of pain.

"OK, okay… all right. Don't break it, goddamn it!"

"Call it a day and sleep it off and I won't break it. This is your last warning."

"All right, man, all right. Just let me go!"

Jason let go. Holding and rubbing his wrist, the guy stumbled to his feet. Jason looked at the man's friends.

"Get him outta here."

They didn't have to be told twice. The harassed hippie girl came over to Tom.

"Wow, who's your friend?"

"Jason… Think I'll call him Mister Jason after that."

"Tell him I'm staying in the white tent. Has the University of Vermont mascot flag in front of it."

"What's that? A moose?"

"No way, a catamount."

"A what a mount?"

"Catamount, you know, the name for any large cat like a mountain lion."

"Maybe I'll call him The Catamount Kid instead."

"Yeah, definitely a lion."

Tom smiled at the girl.

"I'll let him know where you are."

Chapter Twenty-One
Cabot's Wolf Moon Rising
Mountain Festival, Vermont
1974
Free Love

Morning broke. Tara snuggled into his chest. Heavy sleep. No sex. *What, no free love? Nope... But plenty of free pot!* Tara and Tom smoked a joint.

"What's up with the trail these days?"

Tom was quiet. "Gotta finish, Tom."

"Wanna stay here in Vermont... with you."

"Won't work and you know it."

"Oh, and what would Buddha say?"

"'There are only two mistakes one can make along the road to truth; not going all the way, and not starting'... You started your journey and now you must finish it."

"Yeah, well, I found my own Buddha saying... 'Be where you are; otherwise, you will miss your life.'"

"Tom, he's talking about being in the present, the here and now, not about staying in one spot. Why did you start your journey, anyway?"

"I was too protected. In a way, I was living in a palace."

"A palace?"

"Yeah. The people in my palace belonged to private clubs, and private schools, and had nice cars and huge houses. Safe from harm. Safe from hunger. Safe from evil. Every parent was a doctor, lawyer, or some top dog exec. Hell, just down the street lives the CEO of Coca-Cola."

"So, how's the journey going?"

"I'm far more attached to that worldview than I ever realized. I am greedy. Superficial. And egocentric. And that even my hike is a fraud—"

"Fraud, how so?"

"I've taken this trip knowing that deep down inside, I have an insurance policy in my back pocket."

"Oh, and that would be?"

"Tara, at any given point, I can pick up a phone and call my parents. They would rescue me. I could be home and be safe in my palace again within a day. If cops arrested me, I'd have the best lawyers. If I went to the hospital, I'd have the best doctors. If I needed cash, it would be wired to me in a heartbeat."

"Nothing exists alone, Tom. You were dealt a handful of blessings, and you should be thankful. In the end, only three things matter: how much you loved, how gently you lived, and how gracefully you let go of things not meant for you."

"Wait a dang minute, was that a Buddha quote?"

"Of course." They laughed. Hugged. And kissed for the first time. They were locked together.

"There are things I need to learn here. When fall comes, I'll finish my hike. I promise." Tara kissed Tom softly.

"I have to go and do my patrol now," Tom said.

"I'll be here."

*

Everything was quiet now that "Mister Obnoxious" had his butt kicked. Jason came quietly crawling out of the University of Vermont tent. Very quietly.

"Found your hippie girlfriend. Wait, you're sneaking out while she's asleep, aren't you?"

Jason rolled his head and stretched. After a series of yawns, he stretched some more. His haggard eyes told the story.

"I've seen this movie. Jason, you're slipping out on her, aren't you?"

"No, nothing like that."

"OK, so what's her name?"

"Her name?"

"Yeah, who is she?"

"Don't know. Don't care."

"Yeah, why should you? You jumped her bones, so what the hell? Been there, done that, Jason. Let me give you a tip. You're in what I call the horny toad stage."

"Give me a break."

"Yep. You'll chase every young gal, or for that matter, any beautiful Mother you can find."

"Yeah, yeah, so that's your tip? I'm in the horny toad stage?"

"Oh, you want a tip on how to be good at it?"

"That would be nice…"

"OK… Never call a woman by her name when having sex."

"What? Why?"

"Call out the wrong name and you are up shit creek."

"*Hmm*… Hear ya."

"Say, honey, sweetheart, baby, sugar… anything except Mary when her name is Jane."

"I get the point."

The young girl stuck her head out of the tent. She smiled at Jason. "Oh, there you are, Jason."

"Yeah, didn't want to wake you."

"Coming back later?"

"Sure honey, I'll be back."

*

After the festival, cleaning up sucked. There was trash everywhere. Plastic bottles, paper cups, headbands, blue jeans, tennis shoes, empty cans of food, and more. Flies were moving in.

A great time, indeed. Tom tossed an old cotton sleeping bag onto one of the many piles of trash. The piles dotted the meadow. Tall piles. "Let's burn it." Cabot held up a soda bottle. "Guess these plastic things are better than a bunch of busted-up glass."

"Don't burn 'em, they smoke and stink like crazy," Tom said.

"Soon everything will be made of this shit." Jason already had a bucket full of plastic.

The security guys helped. They were not particularly happy about it. Jason's University of Vermont college gal stayed and helped as well.

"OK then, me and the boys are heading out," Jason announced.

"Thanks." Cabot shook Jason's hand. "Not bad, no injuries, no ODs."

"Man, not even a drop of rain."

The young blonde found Jason. "Hello, babe." Jason gave her a quick kiss.

Surely Jason knew her name by now?

"Been looking for you," she said.

"Well, you found me."

She grabbed his hand and squeezed it. "Listen, I've got to tell you something."

"Fire away."

"Jason, these last few days have been a gas." She twisted back and forth, uncomfortably. "Well, no easy way to say this, Jason, but we can't see each other again."

"What? Why?"

"I've got a boyfriend."

"But you said…"

"I know, I feel bad, Jason."

"But…"

"It's been real, but it's over."

They all watched her walk away. Wham, bam. Jason's mouth was agape.

"Well, Jason, looks like you won't need an exit plan." Tom put his hand on Jason's shoulder.

"You don't understand Tom. I… I was starting to dig her."

Cabot pretended to stab himself in the heart. "That gal just dumped your ass."

"You see, Jason," Tom shook his head, "gals can go through the horny toad stage, too."

*

Tom could tell that leaving the festival was hard for Sally. He tried small talk to ease the situation.

"Cabot, look at what Tom gave me. It's a diamond ring! It's going to save my business!"

"So, you're not engaged?" They laughed. The perfect line to make things lighter.

Sally hugged Tom. "Can't thank you enough. I'm delirious with relief!" *Now that's a Sally line!*

"I'll let you know how everything works out."

She headed out with a smile and a wave. Alone at last. Cabot looked like an overused hound dog.

"Don't know about you, Tom, but I'm starving." They made bacon and tomato sandwiches. No mayo. Not worth the weight. They had raw carrots and celery.

"Cabot, I didn't see any of your chairs, tables, or lamps for sale in Sally's or Tara's store."

"People don't usually buy big items. I make small knick-knacks for them. Wooden cake knives, cutting boards, spoons, toothpick holders."

"That's a shame; your woodwork is amazing."

"I sell the serious stuff on consignment."

"Well Cabot, my list is getting longer."

"What list?"

"Things to learn from Cabot's list."

"What's on the list?"

"Besides woodwork, some karate, judo, and cosmic lovemaking."

"Oh, you planning to hang around for a while?"

"For a while, yeah. Promised Tara I would finish the trail. She threw some Buddha quotes at me."

"She knows a lot of em'. It takes years to learn."

"Yeah, I know. Can learn some of the basics."

"Meditation and yoga are most important."

"Oh yeah, they're on the list."

Cabot opened the door. There were those beautiful mountains. Everything is so lush and vibrant. "Assume you'll wait until fall?" Cabot asked.

"Mid-fall."

Cabot stepped out onto the porch. "Well then, let's get to work."

Chapter Twenty-Two
Cabot's Cabin, Vermont
1974
Sacrifice, Discipline, and Love

Months passed. Fall was shaping up nicely. Mid-sixties. But there was rain. Endless rain. Everything was soaked. No matter. They would always follow their daily schedule. It never changed. Seven days a week. Yoga and meditation at sunrise. Length of martial arts sparring sessions. Learning about herbs. Fixing and building things. And woodwork art. Every day was full. And every day was exhausting.

Tara made the trip up every Friday. Stayed until early Monday. She did everything Tom did.

Tom was flat-out in love. Callie seemed like light-years ago. Now, he wasn't really sure he actually loved Jane. She was more of an infatuation. Part of the adventure. Tara was a slap in the face. Full of surprises. How was he to know she was a brown belt in judo? He didn't have a clue she was handy with a bow and arrow. They often competed. Friendly-ish. Clean-up duty was at stake.

"Do you wanna go for a hike?" Tara asked.

"Why not? This rain is nothing more than a little peach juice."

"Peach juice?"

"That's what we call a misty rain in Georgia. The Peach State. What do you guys call a misty rain up here?"

"We call it... a light misty rain."

"Well, duh... how silly of me." Tom rolled his eyes.

"We got lots of names for mud in Vermont. Not so many for rain."

"Must be slippery as hell up here."

"When you are here after a winter, you'll learn all about mud."

"What do you call it at its worst?"

"Pea soup. It's brutal. Much worse than this rain."

"OK, let's take advantage of the good weather. Let's hike up to the guest house."

"Guest house... that used to be an old hog pen?"

"Yeah, that's the one, but Cabot and I cleaned it up. Made it into a nice meditation spot."

"Would rather go to the deck that overhangs the river."

Tom nodded. "OK. We'll go there."

The switchbacks were hell. Full of rocks made slippery by rain. Tom handed Tara the hand-carved walking stick that he recently made. She smiled at him. She smiled at the beautiful carving of a wolf's head.

"The handle is in honor of Wolf Moon Rising."

"The wolf is my spirit animal," Tara replied.

"Perfect. What does it mean?"

"It means I have a strong connection to my intuition."

Tom stopped. They could use a breather, anyway. "What the heck does that mean? OK, totally confused."

"Contrary to popular belief, wolves don't act impulsively. They calculate their moves. Their gut keeps them alive."

"And their pack?"

"They are furiously loyal."

Tom let out a cartoonish wolf howl. "Am I part of your pack, Tara?"

"What do you think?" Tom smiled.

Three more switchbacks until they reached the deck overlooking the river. It was water-logged with all the rain. Rushing water-tagged jagged rocks. The sound was captivating.

Tom sighed. "Time to get on the trail."

"Yes, it's time, Tom."

"Do you think Buddha would be proud?" She laughed.

The sun came out and felt good. A huge rainbow cuddled the mountain range.

"I love you, Tara."

*

It was hard to leave Tara. But it was time. Tom was different now. He listened to nature rather than to the crunching noise of his steps. He observed what was around him. Turning off his internal chat line, he was in the present. The here and now. The air was fresh and clean, and with each breath Tom took, he felt energized. He was happy. Before, Tom was a basket case. Hurry. Hurry. Hurry. His only goal was to finish the trail. *How many miles did I hike? How long did it take? Push it. Faster.* Now, time was irrelevant. If Tom discovered a beautiful area, he would often stay for days. Sometimes longer.

Cabot had taught him well. Wild grapes are ripe after August. There were lamb quarters. Better than spinach! Plantain herbs grow low to the ground and contain many yellow roots. This hearty herb seemed to grow well in any condition. Not only edible, but they were great for bug bites. A nice succulent weed called purslane was quite tasty and juicy. Of course, Tom had learned all about edible mushrooms. There were plenty of puffballs, shaggy mane, chicken of the woods, lion's mane, and honey mushrooms. The occasional wild apples. Treats indeed.

Tom had downsized. A sling bag. A good all-weather sleeping bag and a plastic tube tent. A Buck knife. Hallucinogenic mushrooms. Packs of dried food. A small flashlight. A flint. Water purification tablets. And a fishing line with multiple hooks. Nothing extra.

Rock formations were good protection. Once he found a small cave that was perfect. One problem. A family of red foxes had already claimed it.

Third week and all was well. Until... He put everything in a pile, grabbed his Dr. Bronner's mint soap, and took a bath in a rushing stream. There was something huge rummaging in the bushes. Turned out to be a black bear. He froze in the stream as the bear ate everything in his sling bag. Including his magic shrooms.

Tom had been taking magic mushrooms daily in small doses. No tripping. Low doses floated him along nicely. Revealing intense colors. It led him into the here and now. Luckily, Tom didn't lose all of his shrooms. He had some in his coat pocket. Enough for a few days.

What the hell, at least I still have some.

After the bear was long gone. He chewed on a few of them. Empty stomach. No breakfast. He washed them down with lots of water. Not enough to trip. But strong. No portal. No stopped clocks. No pennies lying around. No strange path to follow. It would be a nice experience. He knew what to expect. It wasn't enough to send him over the edge. No intense hallucinations. No flood of psychedelic shapes, contours, or colors. No, this was going to be like riding in a convertible and feeling the wind in your face. But he would be immersed deeply in nature.

Tom hit the sweet spot with his mushroom high. Almost too much. But not. He sat on a boulder. *Wow, what a great view of the mountains*. His body felt the rhythm of the rock. An ancient drumbeat. *Cool*. A deep groan interrupted him. The bear had come back and was working his way up the mountain. Maybe thirty yards away.

Shit. I bet you're fried by now, fella. How fried, I don't know. The bear circled round and round and round. Snorting at rocks. *Take it easy, pal… take it easy.* He rolled on the ground and then stood. Seemed to be staring at a multicolored tree. *Are you seeing colors? Do things look different?* The bear sat down. Looked at the sky. Yawned. An eternity passed. The bear appeared to be stuck in a trance. Frozen.

"Well, well, laddie."

"Who's there?"

"Don't recognize the voice of an old friend?"

"Pat? Pat, is that you?"

"What's up, laddie?" Pat stepped out from behind a massive rock, shaking his head.

"Holy shit, is that really you, Pat?"

"The genuine article."

"The Pat I remember was a handsome Irishman."

"You never give up, do ya? OK, what's the deal with the wacky bear?"

"That bear is fried."

"Half expected to see him dance with you."

"Pat, gotta say… you show up at the weirdest times."

Chapter Twenty-Three
Appalachian Trail, Vermont
1974
Dreams Do Come True

Twilight of the day. Hiking, yes. Mushroom tripping bears, no. A roaring campfire was a good time to tell Pat about Tara. Tara this, Tara that... and more Tara this.

"Jesus Tom, what is it with this girl? Does she walk on water?"

"What? Pretty much."

"OK, I get the picture. She's the most beautiful woman in the world. A real angel. Communicates without even talking. Never argues."

"Yeah, that's about right."

"You make me want to puke, laddie."

"Puke away."

"She's perfect, is she Tom?"

"Well, she has a chipped tooth, but I think that gives her personality."

"My God, what kind of acid are you on?"

"Why don't we drop talking about Tara? I'll tell you about the others."

"Please do. Hate seeing a young man grovel."

"Grovel? You would too, Pat."

"You're slobbering over this girl."

"OK, a guy named Cabot started training me…"

"Training you?"

"Yes. Every day. Self-defense. Meditation. Woodwork. Herbs. You name it."

"So, you finally got off your ass and started working. All this talk about challenging yourself physically on the trail was—"

"Was what, Pat?"

"Ridiculous. 'I'm going to test my physical will.' Waaaah… You want to test your will, go to war, or go to prison?"

"OK, I get it. Pat, let's just take it easy. Enjoy this cool fire."

Son of a bitch, he's busting my chops. For what?

"Please, go on Tom."

"OK, last try. I'm going to tell you about Sally."

"Sally?"

"Yeah, this cool chick I met in New York. Told her all about you. She thinks you're different from the rest."

"Really, well that's a little spooky. What's the deal with this, Sally?"

"She's a psychic, and she's the real deal."

"A psychic?"

"Yes. She said that you are my spiritual guide."

"Your guide? What the heck?"

"No shit, Pat, she's extremely insightful. Extremely so. She looked right into me. Like I said… she's the real deal, man."

"Laddie, are you sure you want to go there?"

"Yeah, man. But first, let me eat a few more shrooms."

"Good idea."

"Well, aren't you going to bash Sally like you did Tara and Cabot?"

"No, not at all. Just pulling your chain. They sound like pretty good people. Tom, let me tell you something about me. Sally was close, but not quite right."

"I'm listening."

"We've met before."

"Before the trail?"

"Yes. Way back. During your childhood. We played every day."

"I'm confused."

"You had an imaginary friend. Remember? His name was Patty…"

"How did you know that?"

"Tom, you know who I am. You just don't want to accept it."

"Shit… that can't be you…"

"Yes, Tom, I'm the grown-up version of Patty."

Tom's mind raced. A kaleidoscope of memories with Pat flashed in seconds.

Did I dream all of that… Was I hallucinating all that? What's real and what's not?

"Pat, that can't be…"

"I know it's a shock."

"You're telling me you don't exist?"

"What do you think it means that you are the only one that can see me? The only one to ever talk to me? You're the only one to explore with me? Look at me. Look at me. Look hard."

Tom focused. Pat's beard disappeared. Poof. Baby curls of short, flaming red hair appeared atop his angelic face. The beautiful soft child's face of Patty.

"Holy shit!" Tom's inner world shattered. "Holy shit. What's happening to me?" Tom looked away.

"You see me? Don't you?"

"Are you telling me that you're a figment of my imagination?"

"Yes."

I've done way too many shrooms.

Darkness took hold as the sunset. Pat walked down the darkening path back toward the direction he came from.

"Where're you going?"

"Stay the course, Tom. No matter what they try to tell you. You're going to wake up soon."

"Wake up? What do you mean, wake up?"

"You'll find out soon enough. But everything is going to seem upside down, inside out."

"Don't leave."

"Oh, I'm leaving; you just think you need me."

"Don't go, Pat."

Pat strolled into the forest. Faded away. Gone.

Wait, Pat... What do you mean wake up?

Chapter Twenty-Four
Greystone Hospital, Atlanta, Georgia
1974
Back to Reality

Heavy rain and heavy wind whipped and beat the beautiful city of Atlanta. A coma patient was motionless in room 1212 of Greystone Hospital. The sound of a ventilator ruled the room. The patient, Tom Hunt, was stable, but in critical condition.

I hear voices… Tara, is that you? Pat? Cabot? I hear you talking, but I don't see you.

Dr. Patrick Kearney, a teaching neurologist, and a few interns were huddled around the patient, taking vitals, and discussing the case. "It's often underestimated what's happening in the human mind when a patient is in a coma. Time and events get distorted. Most coma patients do hear sounds. They pick up on names, hospital sounds, and music."

"Do they dream?" a thin young intern asked.

"Yes," Kearney answered. "Often when they wake up, they have trouble distinguishing what was real and what was a dream. Had one patient that thought he had gone to war? He described in gory detail slashing up the

Viet Cong. Guess what? He'd never been in the army. Some think they have been to the gates of heaven."

"What about their memory?"

"Depends on a lot of factors. Some people lose their short-term memory and slowly gain it back. Others wake up having created a memory. For others, it was more like a long sleep."

Kearney bloviated for at least the next hour about neural systems. To the students, he was always the professor. A fourth-year resident, Cabot, was assigned to this patient. "Cabot, give his history," Kearney said.

"A male in his early 20s, in excellent physical shape. He was hiking the Appalachian Trail. He was found by the Waynesboro, Virginia police four days ago. He was unresponsive. Slow pulse with high blood pressure. Extreme dehydration. They took him to the hospital in Waynesboro, Virginia. He is from Atlanta. His name is Thomas Hunt."

"Dr. Hunt's son?" the thin intern asked.

"Yes, he is Dr. Hunt's son. He's already aware," Cabot confirmed. "According to the Waynesboro police, they had been investigating a drug ring in the mountains at points along the Appalachian Trail. Arrested them. One of the suspects actually showed them where one of their campsites was. And there was Tom in dangerously bad shape. That's when they found Tom and took him to the hospital. Waynesboro believes the dealers doped him up and left him for dead."

"I wonder what they gave him?" This came from a bright-eyed intern.

"Supposedly LSD and MDA," Cabot replied. Anyway, Tom was relocated to Greystone two days ago. Diagnosis, a drug-induced coma."

"On the bright side, it's still early. Most coma patients will come around within a week," Dr. Kearney added.

"What do we do in the meantime?" a female intern asked.

"Monitor him around the clock. The slightest hint that he's coming around. I want to be notified." Kearney held Tom's hand. "Squeeze my hand, Tom... Good news, he squeezed back. Which means?"

"That his sensory network is functioning," the female intern replied.

"Correct." Kearney pointed to Cabot. "You're on call."

A nurse worked her way into the room. "Well, hello, Tara," Kearney said.

"OK for me to give him a sponge bath?"

"Yes, who's the night nurse?"

"Sally."

"Cabot, Tara, and Sally. Excellent. Got my A-team on this case," Kearney smiled.

*

"Errrrggggh... mmmmmm...Ta... ra..." It was the first noise they heard from Tom.

"Tara, did he just say your name?" Sally asked.

"I think so, Tom... Tom, wake up!" Tom blinked rapidly. A mini convulsion. He ripped off the ventilator.

"I'll get Dr. Kearney!" Sally sprinted out of the room.

"Calm down, Tom. Try not to struggle. The doc will be here any minute." Tara clasped Tom's hands. He twitched and then finally settled down.

"Has he said anything?" It was the doctor.

"We heard groans, and we think he said my name."

"Good, his pupils are reacting to this moving penlight."

"Mmmmm. Ttttttt... aaa... rrrr."

"He's trying to talk. What was the very first thing that happened when he woke up?"

"His eyes blinked rapidly."

"And then?"

"He started convulsing. Then he appeared agitated."

"OK, I think phenobarbital would be best."

Tom slipped in and out of his coma. He occasionally whispered a name. Cabot. Tara. Pat. And more.

*

Kearney was in his office drinking a delicious cup of creamy coffee. A knock on the door caught him mid-sip.

"Come in." Kearney watched as a man walked into the room. He was barely recognizable. His haggard face, dark shadowy beard, unkempt hair, and the dark puffy circles under his eyes told the story of a man under tremendous stress. It was his associate and friend, Dr. Hunt.

"Hello, Steve."

"Pat, I want to thank you for—"

"Happy to help."

Steve gave a weak grin and a short nod. Kearney held up an empty coffee mug. "Yes please, black."

"He's improving every day, Steve."

"My wife and I have been worried sick. I feel helpless. There's nothing I can do. Just sit around and wait."

"I'm hoping Tom will show marked improvement in another day or two, and—"

"And that is the critical part."

"Yes, he'll go through post-traumatic amnesia. He'll be totally confused and disoriented. If he passes through that quickly, he'll have a great chance to recover fully."

"And if he doesn't?"

"After seven days, his prognosis isn't good."

"He'll never be the same."

They locked eyes. It would be severe brain damage. Silence. Kearney drank his coffee, but it had gone cold.

Chapter Twenty-Five
Greystone Hospital, Atlanta, Georgia
1974
Life Is But a Dream

The sunlight slipped through the blinds. Bars of light striped Tom's face. Kearney and Tara were there at his bedside. Tom looked groggy. Disoriented. But awake! A great sign. Lots of slurring. Lots of mumbling. But aware!

"Tom... Tom, do you know where you are?" Kearney asked. Tom licked his lips.

"You're at Greystone Hospital. You know, where your dad works."

"Tara, page Dr. Hunt."

*

Walking, talking, and eating all had to be relearned. Rehab was not Tom's idea of fun. It was downright punishing. But needed.

He had a cool speech pathologist, but the physical therapist was relentless. His speech was definitely improving. His fragile memory had vast gaps but was getting better. Best of all, he did show motor improvement.

One step at a time. You got this. No pain, no gain. That's what his physical therapists kept saying. Screw that.

Physical therapy torture for the morning was done. Mr. Pain, as Tom called his therapist, would be back in the afternoon.

Kearney, Tara, and Tom's parents huddled around him. Mom and Dad were still stressed out.

"Can you recall what happened? What put you in the hospital, Tom?" Kearney asked.

I guess there is no rest for the weary.

"No doc, I still don't remember."

"What's the last thing you remember?"

"Hiking. Vermont."

Steve whispered to Kearney. "No way. He never made it to Vermont."

"Tom, are you sure you made it to Vermont?" Kearney pressed.

"Oh, I was there all right. I stayed for months in a cabin."

"Son," Steve interrupted, "I called Jack…"

"Jack?"

"Your fraternity brother, college roommate, and hiking buddy."

"I know who Jack is, Dad. Why did you call him?"

That ass stole my girlfriend.

"He was the last hiker on the trail with you. When he left you… there was only a week before you were admitted to the hospital. You couldn't have been in Vermont for months."

Tom pointed at Tara. "There was a Tara in Vermont." Tara looked quizzically at Kearney.

"I've never been to Vermont."

Kearney nodded. "Tom, do you know Sally?"

"Yes."

"And Cabot? Do you know Cabot?"

"Yes."

"Do you know a Pat?"

"Yes."

"Doesn't it seem odd that the people you know in Vermont happen to have the same names as us?"

Tom's eyes stared blankly. "What?"

"Tom, this was a lot to take in." Kearney put his hand on his shoulder. "I think you should rest for now."

Kearney stepped out into the hall. The others followed. "You see, he heard the names of the people caring for him. Attached our names to the characters he made up. Created a memory of those characters being with him on the trail."

"His timing is way off," Steve said.

"Time gets distorted. Some think they have been out for months or even years. Tom can't seem to reconcile how unlikely it would be that his friends in Vermont have the same names as we do. When I bring Vermont up, he thinks it's all real."

"Does the Tara in Vermont look just like me?" Tara asked.

"No, we're all different. But I need to dig deeper into the details. That's part of why he's having so much trouble digesting this. From his point of belief, logic, and facts do not matter."

"What happens if he can't reconcile all of this?" Tom's mother asked.

"Well Natalie, we'll cross that bridge when we get to it."

*

A promising breakthrough. Yes, Tom still occasionally slurred his words. Yes, he still needed physical therapy. But he was speaking more and moving more. He was eating solid food.

Kearney asked for details about the trail. The people Tom met. Psychedelic trips. Everything. "Tom, when you go into a coma, time and events can be a tricky thing."

"I know what I experienced, doctor."

"Your timeframe is off, Tom. You talk as if you have been gone for—"

"I was in Vermont!"

"Do you still believe that Tara, Sally, and Cabot were there?"

"Yes. And all the others, too."

"None of it was real, Tom."

"Bullshit!"

"None of it was real. Remember, you can hear perfectly well when comatose. Your consciousness was dealing with the only thing it had. The voices of your caretakers. I called Waynesboro Hospital and all the other names you said that you met were hospital related."

"What? No way!"

"Give me a name."

"OK, Gail."

"Gail is a Waynesboro night nurse."

"Jane."

"Jane is a Waynesboro day nurse."

"Hey, what about the Burno family?"

"Your night nurse here, Sally, read to you almost constantly. It was a mafia-based novel."

"What about Kojack?"

"You mean, Dr. Kojack? Attending physician in Waynesboro."

"Duke, Billy, and Booker?"

"They transported you from Waynesboro to Atlanta."

"Fuck…" Balling his fist, he slammed it on the bedside. "Are you going to tell me that Callie isn't real?"

"No, your parents gave me your background. I know Callie was your college sweetheart. And all the people you have mentioned before, your drug overdose are real."

"Wow. This is surreal."

"I know it's a lot to take in, Tom. We don't have a good handle on what goes on in your head when you're in a coma. Don't worry, there is every indication you'll soon get beyond this."

"So, you're saying I heard these names and built this elaborate story with only my imagination?"

"Yes, that's exactly what I'm saying. You will slowly start to make sense of it all."

Tom stared out the window. Construction everywhere. Men working everywhere.

Vermont was as real as those men!

"Doc, what about the psychedelic trips? In a coma? Explain them?"

"Don't you think you need some rest, Tom?"

"No, I need answers."

"OK then, I believe those trips, as you call them, were really near-death experiences."

"What causes those?"

"There are several theories, but I believe it has to do with the lack of oxygen going to the brain."

"So, doc, you don't believe my visions were mystical experiences."

"No Tom, I don't. The lack of oxygen to the brain caused the hallucinations."

Doc, you won't convince me. They were real!

*

Tom could hear his father and mother chatting with Dr. Kearney and Tara. He pretended to sleep but stayed listening to their whispers.

Let's see what they are planning.

"Can he go home?" his mom asked.

"Hopefully soon, Natalie. First, he needs to get reoriented. He still has trouble with what is real and what is fiction. When he's released, he'll need to see a good psychiatrist."

"Dr. Hunt, we have an excellent psychiatrist lined up to work with Tom. Here is his information." Tara handed Steve a card.

"Thanks."

"No way! I'm not going to a psychiatrist." Tom abruptly spoke up.

His father stepped forward. "So, you are awake? It's time to stop all this foolishness."

"You think I'm a fool?"

"I think you're being self-centered. We've been worried sick about you. It's time to grow up. You need help, son."

Natalie joined in, "Son, was Vermont real?"

"It sure as hell felt real."

"Despite everything that Dr. Kearney has told you?"

Tom looked past her at Kearney.

"Doc, I have another question for you."

"Sure."

"I understand that I heard the names of people around me when I was in a coma. But the sequence of those names doesn't make sense."

"What do you mean?"

"After my college buddies peeled off, the first so-called made-up character was Pat."

"Yes, I remember that."

"Well, you see, Doc, two things bother me about that. First, you were one of the last people I met here at the hospital. So, how was Pat first in the story?"

"My best guess is that your brain held our names in your memory but wasn't capable of creating a story until it recovered enough. When your cortex was healed, it was able to pull the names and create the story. You need to know that may have been totally random."

"*Hmm*. I guess that's possible. But that would mean that the entire story was done in minutes."

"More like nanoseconds," Kearney stated. "What else is bothering you?"

"I've been stumped by this recurring thought."

"What's that?"

"You see, I met Pat before I ran into the drug ring guys. Before I overdosed."

Kearney looked at the others and then back at Tom. He sat down on the edge of the bed. "Didn't you say he was your imaginary friend? That he wasn't real? Tom, did you do any drugs before you saw Pat?"

"Yes, pot and psychedelics."

Clever move, doctor. You didn't break confidentiality.

"There's a possibility the name Pat came up from those hallucinations. The drugs must have triggered it. The name may have transferred to your story."

"So, you did drugs that weren't forced on you?" Tears rolled down his mother's cheeks.

Tom raked his fingers through his hair. Rolled his shoulders a few times. Sighed heavily knowing his parents were going to freak. "Yes, Mom. I'm guilty. I've done drugs. Powerful drugs!"

Great. There's Dad's "I'm so fucking disappointed in you" look. I've seen that look enough times. No, I'll never be you, Dad.

"I think we have pushed this far enough for now. Perhaps Tom needs to rest," Kearney suggested.

"Fine with me."

Visibly shaken, they quietly left the room. Maybe now they will plot their next move. What kind of prescription would Kearney or a psychiatrist suggest? Could he harm himself or others? Would it be better to put him in a rehab facility? How were they going to keep him from doing more drugs?

This isn't going to go well... unless I give them what they want.

He had to say that his time in Vermont was not real. Show interest in developing a career. Buy nice things. Read the newspaper. Talk about what's going on in this world. He starts going to church with his parents.

I think I'm going to puke. But okay, bring it on. You guys throw your plan at me, and I'll throw mine right back at you.

Chapter Twenty-Six
The Hunt Family Home, Atlanta, Georgia
1974
Is This the End Or the Beginning?

Every day, Tom was thankful for being out of the hospital. No more Mr. Pain. No more Dr. Kearney. No more shitty patient food. *Thank God!* But, of course, there was a different price to pay. Now he was stuck visiting a cocky, egoistical psychiatrist once a week. A Harvard medical degree was prominently displayed in the therapy room. The doctor's strong passion for free association and dream analysis was nothing to look forward to. And it would be boring. These sessions could go on for years. *Not a freakin' chance!*

The good doctor put Tom on lithium carbonate. Said it was the "gold standard" in treatment for manic-depressive disorder. Tom didn't like how drowsy the meds made him. And diarrhea sucked big time. Tom stopped taking the stuff. Oh, he lied that he never missed a day.

Tom had learned his lesson. No more honesty attacks. Keep his damn mouth shut. Just play the game. It would have saved him a lot of grief if he had denied the Vermont experience. But no, he was being honest.

His father got him a job at the hospital. He didn't ask if Tom wanted it. Just told him, "Son, you start work Friday night." No discussion. No options. Just do it.

Weekend night shifts as a surgeon's assistant were crazy. The hospital was always slammed. People mutilated in car wrecks. Gun and knife wounds. And there were scheduled surgeries as well.

His job was to hand the surgeon whatever tools they needed. Scalpel, clamps, dissecting scissors, forceps, and retractors, to name a few. A good assistant learns to anticipate what is needed. It was important to snap an instrument into the surgeon's outstretched hand within seconds.

Tom made a few slip-ups. Handed the wrong instruments. Dropped things. Broke the sterile field. But mistakes by Tom were always overlooked. Everyone knew who his father was. What idiot would tongue-lash Dr. Stephen Hunt's kid?

During the week, he was taking pre-med courses. Biology, chemistry, genetics, statistics, and other ball-breaking courses. He didn't want to be there, and he wasn't doing well. But it was all part of the plan.

It felt weird living with his parents. Very weird. Live in their house, live by their rules. OK, he hated it. He was getting restless.

Why not just put me in a straitjacket? It all had to come to a head. And soon.

His father was sitting in an old outdoor lounge chair in the backyard. He was watching Tom do some yoga. Headstands in particular.

"You're going to get an aneurysm."

"What?"

"I said, you're going to bust a blood vessel in your brain if you continue doing that headstand thing."

"OK. Thanks, Dad, I'll take that to heart." *Or not.*

"Grab a rocker off the porch and sit with me for a while. I want to share some good news."

Tom liked to rock, especially when he got anxious. Around his father, he was always anxious. He sat down and rocked away.

"Enjoying your work?"

"Seen some incredible stuff, Dad."

Hmm, this has all the feel of a serious talk.

"What's the most interesting thing you've seen?"

"Wow, that's a tough one. Probably the first time I saw lungs. I was surprised at all the black spots it had. Thought he was a smoker. But the surgeon told me it was the city air, not cigarettes, that did that damage."

"Would you be interested in being a surgeon?"

"Don't think so. Those guys do one surgery after the next. After a while, it feels like you're just slicing up roast beef."

"Even heart surgery?"

"It's more interesting, but I don't know…"

"Well, let me tell you what I've lined up for you."

Oh shit! Lined up? What do you mean, lined up?

"An old friend is the head of the department of medicine at the University of Kentucky."

"Yeah." *I don't like the sound of this.*

"He tells me if you make reasonable pre-med grades and do okay on your admissions test, he'll make sure you get into the school. Staying in school will be up to you."

Tom rocked a bit harder. *This sounds like another no-option deal.* He stopped rocking. He wanted to scream. *Keep calm. Don't show your anger.*

"Dad, I'm just trying to concentrate on one day at a time. To be honest, I feel like I can't breathe."

"Why?" His father was giving him the old "loving-but-concerned" look.

It must be difficult for you, Dad. You try so hard to help me. But this is what you want. Not me. You need to let go, Dad.

"It's hard living here. Don't get me wrong, I appreciate having free room and board. But it's hard to live in my childhood home. I feel like I'm back in high school."

"Listen, it hasn't been an easy ride for your mother and me, either."

"I'm sure I've been a pain in the ass. I know that I'm moody."

"Actually, I'm glad you brought it up. Your mother and I have been talking and we would like to help you get a small condo."

It's happening today. I have to tell him. Focus on blue. It's peaceful.

"Dad, it's deeper than just having my own place."

"I'm listening."

"I want to finish what I started… The trail."

His dad's head dropped onto his chest. "I thought you had finally grown up. You're doing so well, and you have a wonderful future in front of you. Tom, it's time to put that foolishness aside."

"Dad, I'll be lucky if I make Cs this quarter. It's not my thing. And as far as being a physician, to be honest, I don't want to be around sick people all the time."

"So, what's your plan, son?"

"Leave tomorrow. Go back to the trail."

"Just walk away from school?"

"Yes."

"Just walk away from your job?"

"Yes."

"Just walk away from a chance to go to medical school?" Tom's silence was the answer.

"Well, son, are you planning on slipping out and leaving it up to me to tell your mother?"

"No, I want to tell her."

That evening, he helped his mother wash the dishes. He sat her down and told her his plan. She cried. Unable to speak. Unable to stop him. And, yes, he cried too.

Chapter Twenty-Seven
Near the White Mountains, New Hampshire
1974
What Feels Like the End Is Often Just the Start

Old man winter was around the corner. Best to go north to south on the trail, so Tom hitchhiked to Maine. Got on the trail at Mt. Katahdin. Headed south. What a beautiful hike from Maine down through New Hampshire. Probably the best on the trail. With each step, he could feel himself getting closer to Vermont. And getting closer to finding Tara, his Tara, not some nurse Tara.

The morning air was fresh and crisp. So cool he could see his breath. Hiking in the cold was much better than hiking in the heat. Soon, it will be full winter. Snow is right around the corner. Nothing was more peaceful than the mountains with a blanket of snow.

Tom pulled out a tube of cheap peanut butter and a somewhat stale tortilla. *Hmm, a perfect breakfast, a cold peanut butter tortilla wrap.* He pretended the sorry wrap was the classic success meal. A ribeye steak with a baked potato and a martini. Butter, sour cream, and chives. Now that was an imagination!

He was sitting on a large rock overlooking the amazing White Mountains. What a beautiful stretch of trail. He let his mind drift. No rudder. Just anywhere. A quote from Buddha struck him: "Three things cannot be hidden long: the sun, the moon, and the truth." *Soon I will know the truth. Was my experience in Vermont real? Oh, it was real. I know it was.*

Tom got lucky. He found a sign posting the name and directions of a trail angel. Kind people who gave trail hikers time to mend their sore bodies. Shower. Wash clothes. Get food. This trail angel's name was Brandon Mills. He lived nearby.

The directions to get to his small cabin were easy. Tom knocked on the door and waited. A mid-sized man with bushy black hair and a patchy beard opened the door. He was more like a question mark than a man. Curled over and looked at his feet.

"Are you Brandon?"

"Yes, I am. You must be a thru-hiker?" The man smiled and stepped aside. The one-room cabin had a small fireplace. There was a kitchen area, complete with a small dining table and chairs. Talk about spartan.

"Goin' south, I hope?"

"Definitely."

"Well, make yourself at home. Have an outhouse if you need it. Otherwise, pull yourself up a chair. I was about to cook some fresh venison. You interested?"

"You bet. I'm starving."

"So, you're doing the trail."

Tom told him that he had already done a good portion of the trail. He just wanted to finish what he had started.

"Plan to stop at Wolf Moon Rising. It's a mountain in Vermont."

"I've done the trail in Vermont; can't say I remember Wolf Moon Rising."

"Brandon, it's not on an official mountain. The owner named it that."

Brandon's wood stove would do the job on the venison.

"The best part of venison is the backstrap." Brandon held up a piece.

"Looks great to me. Am I drooling yet?"

"Got some carrots and bread with it." Brandon pointed to a container on the table. "I boil water if you're thirsty."

Tom filled his canteen about a quarter. He took a sip. It was clean and fresh.

"So, what's your trail name?" Brandon asked.

"Never got one."

"What? You don't have a trail name?"

"Nope. Sure, don't."

"Well, dang man, I'll have to give you one before you leave here. Maybe after I know you better."

"Did you hike the trail?"

"Yes, back in the 60s."

"Trail name?"

"Blue Hiker."

"Why Blue Hiker?"

"Because when I get cold, I turn blue."

They ate venison and carrots. Cooked crispy on the outside and rare on the inside. Steakhouses call it black and blue.

"God bless it, this is good," Tom said.

"Yeah, melts in your mouth!"

"So, why are you up here, Brandon?"

"To get away. I don't fit in, if you know what I mean?"

"I can relate."

"Served in Nam. I was just a grunt on the front lines, but I have seen what people can do to each other."

"I'm sorry."

"Thought I would be coming home to a hero's welcome. But people spit on me at the airport in San Francisco. They cursed me for trying to protect their freedom. I knew I would never belong."

"Spit on you?"

"That was inside the terminal. Outside, I got hit with eggs and rotten tomatoes."

"Don't know what to say, Brandon."

Brandon's eyes glossed over. "Hell, I've done enough talking about me. How about you, Tom? What brings you this way?"

Brandon was a far better listener than his flaky Harvard psychiatrist ever was. So easy to talk with him. No judgment. Out of nowhere, Brandon pulled out a joint and smiled. Tom smiled back. They sat by the small fireplace to smoke.

"Damn Brandon, this is some badass weed. Is it Colombian?"

"Better, Oaxacan Gold!"

"You old hippies have your sources."

"You know, Tom, I've been thinking about those psychedelic visions you were talking about and the doctor telling you they were near-death experiences?"

"Yeah, go on."

"When I was in Nam, I saw soldiers die and come back to life. Lots of them said the same thing. They saw the 'other side.'"

"So, you think mine were near-death experiences? Didn't really happen?"

"Didn't say that. What I meant to say was… I believe there is something more than just this world. Hell, maybe there are endless different places within this universe. My question is… can you exist in more than one at a time?"

"That's pretty trippy, Brandon."

"It sure is. But as you get older, you do tend to think about what's next."

They sat back in their creaky chairs. Presently, they smoked another joint. Laughed their asses off.

"Brandon, why are you really up here?"

"*Hmm*, well… I'm dying, Tom."

"What? What's wrong?"

Brandon rubbed his knees and then crossed his arms. "I was in the hell of Nam fighting in their vicious jungles. Guerrilla warfare. Worse than any nightmare."

"How long were you there?"

"Two years. Anyway, a general came up with the bright idea to irradicate the bush."

"Agent Orange?"

"Yep, they called it 'Operation Ranch Hand'. Sprayed nineteen million gallons of Agent Orange over 4.5 million acres."

"Wow!"

"Yeah, it's a mixture made of two herbicides: 2, 4, 5-T and 2, 4-D. Whatever the hell that shit is."

"Heard it was wicked shit."

"Yeah, got sprayed more than once. The big C-123s flew over and dumped it. It was like rain, Tom. We'd grab our ponchos and go."

"What the hell?"

"We knew exactly what this stuff would do."

"Shouldn't you be in the hospital?"

Brandon shook his head. "Hell no."

"Maybe they could help you. At least ease your discomfort."

"Tom, I had a black Lab once. We called him Midnight. He was a good one, too. Anyway, one day he lit out after a big fat squirrel. He chased it across the road. He made it. Midnight didn't. He got hit by a truck, Tom. Hit really hard."

"Did he die?"

"Well, eventually. He lived through the initial impact, but by the time I got down to him, the driver told me old Midnight limped off."

"Did you find him?"

"No. Tom, I think he crawled off to die."

"Is that what you're doing, Brandon?"

"That's it in a nutshell. I don't want tubes and crap stuck all over me."

"Are you afraid?"

"It doesn't matter. It's so painful… I pray to die." Brandon put a nice limb on the fire. The fatigue on Brandon's face is shown eerily by the orange glow of the fire.

"You ready to hit the sack?" Tom asked.

"Yes… As Sergeant Joe would say, 'Boys, it's time to get horizontal, belly up.'"

"See ya in dreamland."

Brandon was half asleep when he said, "Your trail name… Hawk Spirit."

Hmm, Hawk Spirit… "Why?"

"Hawk, because they see what others can't see. Spirit, because you see a different world."

Chapter Twenty-Eight
White Mountains, New Hampshire
1974
When You Come Off the Trail, You're Not the Same Person That Went In

Two days later, Tom decides to leave. Saying goodbye was hard. Very hard. Tom felt shitty for leaving Brandon.

Man, Brandon was dealt a bad, bad hand. Dying alone. Should I go back? Did Brandon have a family? Anyone?

No thunder, no lightning, just rain splattering all around. And soon, the mud.

Damn it! Stop thinking about him! No going back.

Brandon had pointed out a good place for supplies. *Focus and get there.*

The rain came down a bit harder. Thumbing will be a bitch. No one will pick up an obvious disaster like me. *Sloppy. Wet. Smelly. Dirty.* A beautiful hemlock was the perfect shelter. The tree was so close to the road that the roots were cracking the pavement. Drivers can't miss him.

Two cars. No luck. Not even a slowdown. Thank God, a big truck pulled over. He motioned for Tom to get in. The driver sported a New York Yankees cap. He seemed pleasant enough. Except he had fidgety fingers and looked down as he talked.

"Where ya heading?" The man sounded friendly.

"Heard there was a town nearby?"

"No, no town. Just some stores at a four-way stop."

"That'll work." Something didn't feel right.

"So… you're a Yankees fan?"

"Yeah. Been to a few games. Love watching Joe Torre. And you?"

"Braves! And I'll match your Torre with Davey Johnson and Darrell Evans and raise you with a Hank Aaron."

He turned off his truck. "Mind if I just sit for a little while? Been driving since sunrise."

"Not at all. What's your name?"

"Jimmy. But my friends call me Road Rat."

"Road Rat?"

"Yeah, 'cause I'm on the road all the time and I haul metal salvage. Mostly junk cars… So, what's your name?"

"Tom."

"Yeah, but ya got a trail name?"

Don't think you would understand my trail name.

"Still working on it."

"I'm sure it'll come to ya."

"Yeah, it will."

"Need to drop this load off. It's a little out of the way. After that, I can take you to the four-way. You okay with that?"

"Sure. No rush," he said innocently.

They carried on quite a gabfest. Sports. Music. And of course, women.

"This is my place."

A big graveyard of crushed cars was stacked four feet high. Dishwashers and dryers. Metal bars and pipes. Gutters and downspouts. All kinds of scrap.

Road Rat's job was crazy dangerous. Just like him. There was a huge metal crusher that could swallow cars. No telling what it could do to a man. Massive shredders. Grapples. And a magnetic separator.

"What do you think of my toys, Tom?"

"They look scary as hell."

"Only a couple of loads. Watch this shit…"

Wham! Metal on metal violently crunching and smashing. Steel bars and a refrigerator slammed into the machine. A screeching sound slowed the engine. Clunk! Dead silence. The cruncher was jammed!

"Son of a bitch… third time this week." Road Rat went to a shed and came back with a fifteen-pound sledgehammer.

"That looks like it will do the trick." Tom laughed.

Bam. Bam. Bam. Nothing. "All right, gotta call my repair guy. Let's get the hell out of here."

"You were scaring the bejesus out of me. You were standing on the side of the grinder, hitting it with a freakin' sledgehammer. If it had opened, you would have fallen right in."

"Ah, do it all the time." Road Rat cranked the massive truck again and headed down the road.

Wait a damn minute. This wasn't the way we came in.

"Where're we headin'?"

"Just down the road a bit. You gotta see this view."

His stomach knotted up. The truck stopped. There was a view of a gorgeous river, mountains, and waterfalls.

"What do ya think of this view?" Road Rat asked.

"Breathtaking."

"Sorta romantic? Don't you think?"

"This is where you bring your girlfriend?"

"I would, if I had one. They aren't my style."

Oh shit.

"So, Tom, what's the ride worth to ya?"

"What, you want money?"

"No, something more personal." Road Rat undid his belt and then looked at Tom.

"No way, man. I'm not that way."

"Never had me a southern boy." His hot hand was on Tom's thigh. "How about twenty bucks? A runaway like you always needs cash. What do you say?"

"Think I'll pass." Tom opened the door.

A large hunting knife flashed. He grabbed Tom's collar. "I'm not gonna ask you again. Blow me really good, or I'll cut you up like a spring chicken."

Tom grabbed Road Rat's finger and bent it backward, almost breaking it. Another inch and it would shatter.

"Jesus!" Road Rat screamed with pain. "Stop, goddamn it, please stop."

"Throw your knife out."

The man frantically lowered his window and tossed the knife. "OK… okay already. I got rid of the fuckin' knife."

"What else do you have? A gun?"

"No… no, I swear I don't. Please, please stop."

Tom reached over and took the keys to the rig. "You try to follow me; I'll tear you a new asshole. Understand?"

His head bobbed up and down rapidly. "Yes, I got it. I got it."

Tom released his hold on the finger and opened the truck door. He hit the ground, heaved the keys as far as he could, and took off. He found a good spot to hide and watch. Road Rat looked around frantically for his keys, cursing steadily. "Goddamn it, here they are."

No more thumbing today.

Tom was pissed that he was caught off guard. *Should have listened to my gut*. But how did he know that self-defense hand move? It was so deliberate. So fast. *Cabot taught me that move*. Thousands of repetitions made it instinctual. *That's right, Cabot taught me. How could a dream, Dr. Kearney, teach me that move?*

It was pleasant hiking down the road. No more rain. Clear sky. A couple of trucks passed him. One good Samaritan stopped. Tom waved him on.

At last, he saw a few stores. Cars were packed in front of a restaurant. He appeared to be on time for a late lunch.

The quaint stores and the one restaurant were named Little Oasis. Little Oasis gas station. Little Oasis restaurant. Little Oasis grocery store. He went into the restaurant. It was still practically full. Truckers, drivers, and farmers. The food smelled wonderful.

"Today's blue-plate special is meatloaf and mashed potatoes. Would ya like something to drink?" A thin lady with a name tag that read, 'Betty' asked. She was probably in her 60s.

"Iced tea would be fine."

"Sweet or unsweet?"

"Half and half?"

"Sure can, honey. You know what you want?"

"Betty, can you tell me more about that blue-plate?"

"You'll love it. Everything is homemade. Today is our meatloaf with the best BBQ glaze you've ever tasted. Garlic or regular mashed potatoes. And your choice of green beans or peas?"

"Sounds like the ticket. I'll take the garlic taters and the peas."

"Need anything, just let me know."

The man who approached him was not smiling. "Hello, I'm the manager."

"Pleasure to meet you."

"You're the hitchhiker that just came off the trail, aren't you?"

"Yes. Sorry, I'm so wet and dirty."

"A trucker wearing a Yankees baseball cap stopped here for an early lunch. Told me all about you."

"Oh?"

"Yeah, he said you tried to rob him."

"What?" Tom shook his head. "I tried to rob him?"

"Yeah, you were thumbing. He picked you up. You pulled out a knife as soon as you got in the truck. Threatened to cut him up like chicken fricassee."

"That's bullshit, mister. He pulled a knife on me."

"Why would he pull a knife on you?"

"He wanted something else from me."

"Something else?"

"Yeah, something I wouldn't give."

"Well, it's none of my business either way. I can tell you don't plan on robbing my store. But just in case, I've got a double-barrel shotgun right here under this classic old-timey register, and believe you me, I know how to use it."

"I'm not robbing anybody, mister. That guy flat-out lied through his miserable teeth. He still here?"

"No, he took off after he ate." His stern look gave a clear message. 'I've got an eye on you' kind of message.

Tom motioned to the waitress. "How about a large salad with that special?"

"Sure thing. What kind of dressing?"

"Got any recommendations?"

"The Concord is my favorite. Maple syrup, red wine vinegar, shallots, and a couple of secret ingredients. I tell ya, it's awesome."

Cabot shoveled his food down and even ate some cherry pie for desert.

"Everything was awesome. So was the glazed meatloaf." Tom handed the manager the bill, just under five dollars. He tossed down a ten. "Give the change to Betty."

The manager took a long, uncertain look at Tom. "The guy said he kicked your ass."

"Do I look like a guy who got his ass kicked?"

"Well, not exactly."

"Now who's telling the truth?"

The man became at ease. *Wouldn't be needing that shotgun today.*

"Where's the closest hotel?"

"Just around the corner to the right. The Little Oasis Motel. It's not much, but the truckers don't complain."

Little Oasis Motel... That's a shocker. "Why didn't they build it on that open corner of the four-way?"

"It was built five years before they paved the four-way. Otherwise, my brother would have."

Tom nodded "OK… I'll be back for breakfast."

Chapter Twenty-Nine
Near the White Mountains, New Hampshire
1974
The Ugly Side

The Little Oasis Motel was no Oasis. Repugnant smells throughout. Old cigarettes. Stale sweat. Mildewed carpets. There was a rust stain in the toilet. And the shower grout was slimy and moldy. Bedbugs? Probably. *Not crawling in that damn bed tonight!*

He slept in his sleeping bag on top of the bed.

What was that freakin' noise now? Sounds like two people are hard at it. Wham! Bam! Wham! Bam! *Is this going to go on all night?*

He barely stopped himself from kicking the wall.

Wait it out, Tom. Wait it out. It'll stop soon.

He looked outside. The parking lot was full of trucks of all kinds. In particular, he noticed there were no metal salvage trucks. *Thank God. Enough drama for one day.*

A citified dude was leaning against his Lincoln Continental. He was wearing a large tan overcoat with a fur collar. A wide-brimmed hat made his head look small. Smoking a big fat black cigar.

Why not wear a sign? I'm a pimp, right here.

Tom watched as a trucker and a lady stepped outside just below Tom's room on the first floor.

"Sweetheart, that was the best ever!" A euphoric, starry-eyed trucker screamed. He waved a half bottle of Jack at her.

"Yeah, call me again and I'll show you some more. Haha." She was a fox. Short red miniskirt. Platform super high heels. She hot-footed to the blindside of the Lincoln and handed the cash to the pimp. Tom stepped outside. Their voices carried toward the hotel.

"Brush your hair and hit Room 226. Guy wants the deluxe package."

She stayed put. Hand on her hip, she whispered something to him. The pimp pulled out a small bag and handed her a bill to snort with. He gave her a couple of lines.

"Buttercup, there's more blow after your next John."

"What room?"

"226. Near that dude standing outside his door. See him?"

"Yeah."

"Stroll by him and see if you get a bite."

The handrail kept her upright as she clumsily climbed the stairs and walked toward Tom. She had doe-like eyes and heavy, caked-on makeup she didn't need. She reeked of perfume that left a lingering trail.

"Good evening," Tom said.

"Stop by on my way back?"

"Sorry, have a girlfriend."

"Promise I won't tell."

"Thanks, but no thanks."

How did she walk in those ridiculous high-platform shoes? She had a thousand-watt smile. *Why is a woman like her doing this?*

He made room on the balcony for her to leave. The door next to his room opened, closed, and reopened.

"No baby, you can't keep me any longer. I'm very late as it is." The woman said as she brushed her hair with a wide toothcomb.

"Come back, baby." A deep voice echoed out.

"No, I'm already in trouble."

Tom moved aside as she made a quick escape. She lightly bumped into him. A cinnamon brown boho dress echoed her eyes. A tangled-up flaming red wig told the story of her night. She straightened her rumpled skirt. "Waiting for me?"

"No, I've been staying in the room next door. You know, the one with the thin walls."

She shrugged. Totally aloof. Totally clueless.

Bullshit. You scream like an alley cat.

She hurried down the stairs and out to the car. She nervously handed the pimp the cash.

"Hell, bitch! You let that punk trucker eat up your night. This all you got for it?"

He raised his hand for a serious slap, but held back. A dwarfish, squirrely-faced trucker was crossing the lot. "Try looking sexy for this, dude. He may be your next John."

Man, he looked worn out, dragging his duffel bag toward the motel. The floozy cut him off, towering over him. "Hey honey, you want some fun tonight?"

He looked her up and down. "How much?"

"How much fun do you want?" Her massive breasts were at his eye level.

"*Fun*... How about real fun?"

"Yeah... well, a hundred can make that happen."

"Hundred? I don't think so. Seventy max."

She looked at the pimp. He gave her a cold thumbs up.

"OK, sounds good."

Now squirrely face was heading to happy land. The pimp... Big man. Big hat. Big cigar. Big mean bastard. Bet you're a badass gorilla pimp. Take all their money, don't you? Fuck you.

An old night manager turtle walked out to the Lincoln. *Getting a cut to turn a blind eye, aren't you, pal?*

He joined the pimp. They laughed it up a bit.

"He'll be here in a few," the manager said.

"Man, that bastard is robbing me blind."

"Yeah, but you're safe."

"Safe as long as he needs my money. If he gets a better deal somewhere... He'll come after me faster than a hungry mountain lion."

"Naw, man, he's my cousin. He wouldn't double-cross me."

"If you say so."

A New Hampshire State patrolman whipped into the lot and stopped next to them. The pimp reluctantly went to the patrolman's window. He waited for him to lower it and handed over an envelope. They bumped fists.

So much for the cops.

The lights of the cop car faded down the street.

All right, game on.

Tom calmly approached the pimp, although inside he was anything but calm. He was so nervous a good puke would probably make him feel better. *Would the pimp grab a tire iron? Would he pull out a knife or a gun?*

"Good evening."

The pimp tossed his cigar to the ground. Ground it out with his shoe. He was silent.

"Wanna line me up a girl?"

"Seen you up there watching me, mister. I get pissed when somebody spies on me. Real pissed."

"Wasn't spying."

"Yeah, what would you call it?"

"Just admiring one of your gals."

"Which one? Running five of them tonight."

"She's wearing a red miniskirt."

"Yeah, sweet. Best in my stable." The pimp grinned.

"How much?"

"For her? Like I said, she is the most popular."

"Fifty?"

"Gotta do better than that, man. Like I said, she's the queen."

"Don't have more."

"Bullshit, slick. You want the girl or not?"

"All right. I'll toss in another ten." Tom sighed.

"Ten?"

"OK, twenty."

The pimp smiled, flashing a bright gold grill. "What room?"

"230."

"She'll knock four times on your door."

Tom backpedaled from the pimp and went upstairs to his room. He waited. And waited. Almost fell asleep. A soft, repeating knock on the door. He opened it to find the girl there, fluffing out her chest.

"Decided to have a little fun, after all?"

"Why not?"

"Have anything to drink?"

"Ah, no, sorry."

"Any good drugs?"

"Just weed and some…"

"Oh, hell no! That shit just makes me sleepy."

"And some really potent LSD."

"No, Big Poppa would be pissed."

Big Poppa… There you go. How sweet. Provides for ya just like a Daddy.

She walked into the room, kicked off her heels, and unbuckled her thick black leather belt.

"Wait! Uh, let's talk." Tom held up his hand to slow down.

"Talk? Got a wimp weenie or something?"

"No, no, nothing like that."

"Fast on the gun?"

"No… don't think so."

"Yeah, well, don't care, anyway."

"Slow down. I want to find out a few things."

"Oh, that's it. Well, I don't have the clap or anything like that. Get tested often, so don't worry. I'm not spreading anything but my legs. Haha."

"No," Tom backed up a step, "just want to talk for a little while."

She dropped her head and sighed heavily. "Oh no, you're one of those… Well, I don't give my life history. Don't tell people how I got into this business. Don't tell them about the business. And I hate small talk."

"Listen, I want to help."

"Help me? Well, isn't that special? You and every other swinging dick. I'm not gonna run away with you. Not gonna be your girlfriend. Don't want your help. All I want is my money. Stiff me, and Big Poppa will pistol-whip your ass. Understand?"

"Yeah, here are three twenties and a ten."

She put her heels, earrings, and coat back on and picked up her bag. "Don't waste any of the other girls' time, either. They're just like me. Don't want no help." In a huff, she marched out, cursing under her breath. At the stairs, she shouted, "Big Poppa, he's a punter with a big yap." She storms off, cussing Tom, and rejoined her pimp.

Trying to help people is not so easy. I wonder if Tara has a Buddha quote for this!

Chapter Thirty
White Mountains, New Hampshire
1974
Are Dreams Also Reality? Don't Know, Do You?

A light dusting of snow. So quiet. Eerily quiet. It's the perfect time. The perfect time to enjoy a little windowpane acid. Not too much. *There ya go. That should give me a kick-ass high.*

A wide stream soon blocked his path. Not too deep, only about knee-high. No way to jump rocks. *Should I try the slippery birch log? Might be a good bridge.*

What the hell? You got this. He thought putting one foot in front of the other would work. Except he fell halfway across into the cold water.

"Goddamn, that water is cold!" He could barely get his breath... *Jesus!* He was completely soaked to the bone. His right leg was throbbing with pain. *Oh shit.* He had to commando crawl. He pushed over to the bank with his good leg. He tried to stand, but his leg said no way. It was too damp and muddy to camp here. Now the acid was kicking in.

Thank God. Don't fight nature... Go with the flow.

Should have waited for the high. Bet I'd still be dry if I did. Maybe. What the hell?

In the distance, Tom thought he heard a man singing. It was getting closer. Deep voice. He recognized an old Irish pub song. It was getting louder and closer.

What will we do with a drunken sailor?
What will we do with a drunken sailor
What will we do with a drunken sailor?
Early in the morning!
Shave his belly with a rusty razor
Shave his belly with a rusty razor
Shave his belly with a rusty razor
Early in the morning!

"Hey! Help... I need help over here!" Pat appeared from behind the bushes.

My God, you got to be kidding me.

"Well now, it looks like you are in a fine fix, laddie. Sorta cold to be going swimming, don't you think, Tom? Or were you washing your filthy clothes?" His ever-present sarcasm was still present.

"Nonsense. A cold dippy is good for circulation."

Pat handed Tom his walking stick. "You added another head below the first one and they're identical."

"Figured if one wood spirit was good, then two would be even better."

"Whatever you say, spirit man... Set up camp near here?"

"Staying at the Trapper John Shelter. It's a wonderful accommodation just a few bends away. The shelter has three walls. A tall chimney a few yards in front of the shelter. It was an old cabin, and the coolest part was that the chimney whistled in the wind. Such a pleasant sound to relax with. A luxurious outhouse just behind that tree. Bring your own paper."

"Sounds delightful! I'll take the room overlooking the waterfall."

"Excellent choice."

The first order of business for Tom was to make a good fire to dry his clothes. He hobbled over to the nearest trees and tied a string between them to make a clothesline.

"Pat, where the hell did you go? Last time I saw you, you just disappeared."

"Let's just say I went to another place and bounced back from it."

"What made you bounce back?"

"You."

"Me?"

"You called; I came, laddie."

"I didn't call you."

"Oh yes, you did. Let's just call it spiritual intuition."

"Bullshit."

"It's the truth. Besides, you can use a bit of help."

"Can you fix a bum leg?"

"My ancestral line is tied to Dian Cecht. He was a healer, both physically and spiritually."

"What?"

"Tis true."

"Pat, according to my doctor, you don't exist!"

"Well, that's not true now, is it, Tom? Do you hear me? Do you see me? Don't I help you?"

"This is crazy; I'm talking to myself."

"Crazy as in deranged, no. Crazy as in demented, no. Crazy as in you're wildly aggressive, no."

"How about therapist-certified crazy? The kind of crazy that doctors give meds to zap hallucinations. That kind of crazy."

"Think about it, Tom. Most people wish they would learn to listen to themselves. You have a gift, not a curse. And you'll heal yourself if you listen to me…"

"OK, I give up. Crazy or creative; what difference does it make?"

"There you go, laddie buck." Pat handed Tom some smooth, colorful rocks.

"What are they?"

"Healing rocks. Pick one and rub on it. You see, I have the power similar to Dian Cecht…"

"Yes, you told me that already."

"Well, what I am saying is that power is actually within you. The name Dian means swift, and the name Cecht means power."

"So, you're telling me I have a swift power for healing?"

"Hey, remember the saying, *medice, cura te ipsum*?"

"Huh?"

"Latin for physician, heal thyself."

"I don't know Latin!"

"You do. You just don't know that you know it."

"OK, okay, enough with that!"

Tom checked his clothes to see if they had dried. Nope, still damp. He put his hands close to the fire and rubbed them.

Translucent orange-red crystals came out of Pat's pocket next. "Beautiful crystals." Tom smiled.

"Carnelian crystals."

"What do they do?"

"Boost circulation." Pat wrapped the crystals and placed them on Tom's knee.

"OK, you're the boss. I'll go with the flow."

"Give me some food; I want to mix some Irish sea moss with it. Red moss has a lot of benefits, especially anti-inflammatory."

"Here, mix this Tang with some water."

"It'll fix your *gotaigh*... rather, your injury."

"So, it will cure my injury? Well, I'd rather it remove the *pian san asal.*"

"I'm not a pain in the ass! Laddie, do you know you're speaking the old Irish language?"

"Damn, how?"

"Tom, there are eons of knowledge within you. What you learn in your lifetime and what you carry from your ancestral pool. Now you need to unleash it."

"Is that what shrooms do? Unleash my power? Because I am buzzed out of my mind. Flat out zooming."

"Someday you won't need them."

"Don't know about that. But I do know Tang with sea moss tastes like shit."

"That it does, laddie. You'll be skipping down the trail. Especially if we toss in a few chants."

"Chants? I don't feel like chanting right now, or anytime soon."

At last, his clothes were dry, he was so happy to feel them on his body.

*

Big flakes of snow. Huge flakes. Would be a slippery and difficult morning on the trail. Best to stay put. His leg was better. Much better. His trail buddy sat by a stoked-up fire smoking a pipe and drinking herbal tea.

"Did you carve that pipe?"

A thick, blueish smoke ring accompanied a firm, "Yep."

"Wow, very strange."

"What?"

"Pat, I dreamed about a pipe last night!"

"*Hmm*, what a coincidence. How's the knee?"

"A lot better. No real pain. A little stiff. So, I think I'll stay put and give it another day."

What was that smell? Tom pulled smoke toward his face. Smelled delicious. "What kind of tobacco is that? Smells like… hot pancakes with maple syrup."

"Ha. It's an interesting blend. Called Autumn Evening."

"Makes me hungry." Tom smacked his lips.

"You're welcome to some."

"Nah, I'll pass. It never tastes as good as it smells."

"Know what it means… dreaming about a pipe?"

"No, what?"

"Describe it."

"I was on the trail and so was the pipe. Sitting on a stump. Examined it very closely."

"Studied it long and hard?"

"Yep."

"Might mean calm your ass down a bit. Don't make impulsive, reckless decisions."

"Good advice, Pat. It was a sturdy wooden pipe with a carving on the front of it."

"Carving? What kind of carving, Tom?"

"An old 1800s warship, cannons, and all. Sails puffed out full of wind."

"Means danger or, maybe, opportunity…"

"In the end, I threw it away as far as I could."

"*Hmm*," Pat emptied his pipe, "you gotta decide which way you are heading. To save your spirit, so to speak. Be prepared to be tested. Personal sacrifice may very well be involved."

"All that from a pipe dream, Pat?"

"What do you think?"

"Don't know if you were interpreting the dream, or do you just know me that well…"

Chapter Thirty-One
Green Mountains, Vermont
1975
Set Your Mind Free

Know what's a damn beautiful sight? Glastenbury Mountain in Vermont. The mountain bordering the Bennington Triangle. A good starting point to begin his search. His search for home... Wolf Moon Rising.

Tara was so close... but he had problems galore. The snow was deep. Slogging through this stuff was brutal. His makeshift snowshoes sucked. Everything seemed to take forever. The days were short, and the conditions were hard. The most serious problem was food. Slap out of supplies. Saw rabbits, ducks, and bony squirrels. But they all refused to be captured.

So close to finding Cabot's cabin. No turning around now. His home was just over the next slope. Or the next. The days just stacked up. Plenty of water. But man, he needed calories. He stumbled as he pushed forward. He was dizzy. *It's close. So close. I know it is.*

"It's in this area? You're sure?" Pat asked.

"Yeah, I believe it's here."

"From that ridge up there, we could see the whole valley."

"Need a good rest first. That's a steep-ass mountain."

"You need food even more. This is crazy, Tom."

"Been told that before."

"How long do you think you can go without food?"

Strong, loud sniffs. Pat hovered inches from his face. A few more sniffs.

"What the hell?" Tom pushed Pat's face away.

"Your breath, laddie."

"What about it?"

"It stinks, that's what."

"Out of my face, man!"

"Wow… what a terrible, noxious smell."

"What the hell does that mean?" Tom asked.

"It's like the smell of nail polish remover."

"And?"

"Your body is burning your stored fat. It's a dangerous sign."

"Trying to scare me, Pat."

"Is this some kind of hunger strike?"

"Back off!"

"I know why you're doing this."

"I said back off!"

"You're doing this for spiritual reasons. You want a vision. Something so drastic it will—"

Tom spun and screamed as he smashed his staff against a tree. His scream was spine-chilling.

"Easy, laddie. Don't waste your energy."

"Yes, I've got to find Tara."

"I know, I know. Calm down for a minute. Let's take a look from the ridge."

To Pat, the desperation on Tom's face as he searched for Tara was heartbreaking. Once on the ridge, Tom scanned the area. Total disappointment. Nothing.

"Let's give it up for today, Tom."

They had a good, sheltered campsite. But a freakin' cold night proved they were wrong. Shivering and painfully hungry. The night was long.

Thank God for the morning. The morning sun was glorious. The mountains were smothered with another fresh foot of snow.

Damn, I need to piss. Tom wrapped his sleeping bag around himself. He stepped away from the tent. Liquid relief. Backed away. Smiled at the steaming letters *TARA,* he had made. He chuckled to himself.

Evergreens can provide good comfort. A big one was calling him. A perfect place to sit.

Calming thoughts. How about some blotter? He pulled out a small sheet of blotter acid. LSD saturated on blotter paper. Divided into small, beautiful squares. Tabs, they were called. Each tab was a dose. Each tab was decorated with a small orange sun. Each tab was about the size of the end of a matchstick. One orange sunshine and you're guaranteed a good trip. Strong hallucinations. Profound connectivity.

For a heroic dosage, double the amount. Tom took three. He waited with high anticipation high. *All right, there you are.* He tried to swat the butterflies away from his stomach. Then he took three more.

Loud crunching steps came toward him. "What are you doing, Tom?"

"Took some acid."

"That will help you find her?"

"Maybe, Pat... just maybe."

"How much did you take?"

"A lot..."

Pat rubbed his long red beard. A rock jutted out from the ridge just a few yards away. Pat sat down.

"Do me a favor, Pat."

"What's that?"

"Just don't sing." They burst out in righteous laughter.

"What do you mean trippin'? You'll love my divine voice."

"Pat, there's not enough acid for that."

"Maybe not my voice, but maybe the sound of this flute I made for ya."

"Flute? I don't know anything about flutes."

"That may be. But, then again, who knows when you are flying so high?" It was a simple wooden flute. Only six holes.

"Pat, I'm just starting to trip my ass off." It was vision time.

*

Solid objects were fluid. Trees were breathing, and the snow was brighter, puffier, and dancing in the sky. Each flake had its energy; blue, green, yellow, and red flakes slowly merged with the ground. A white glacier is what he saw. Joyous music played. He closed his eyes, inhaled, and exhaled deeply. He was floating. *Wow, I'm flying.* He soared to the top of the trees. Jetted to the far side of the valley. What freedom! Tom could see his body sitting peacefully. Wrapped in his sleeping bag. The portal appeared. It was covered in snow.

I recognize you. Now I know I'm in the right place.

He waited. The door cracked open. The disturbing sound of steel grinding. The weather was much the same. Such colorful snowflakes. A path untouched by the snow. He remembered he was flying, so he went flying down the path. There was a tunnel. It was pitch black... Just a speck of bright light shone at the end of the tunnel, so to speak.

"I know an easier way," a ragged voice said. A pasty-skinned old man stood behind him. Uncombed white hair and beard. It flowed down the front of his hooded white cloak. Blended him right into the snowy background. "I said, know an easier path to take."

"Not looking for the easy path; I'm looking for the path that will lead me home."

The old man continued, "Horrible things have happened in this tunnel, son. Something very evil lives there."

"You're not scaring me."

"I bet; have you heard of Hades?"

"No," Tom replied.

"He's a demon. This is his *tunnel to nowhere.* Go in, never come out."

"Thanks for the warning, but I'm taking the path."

Tom felt his way into the darkness. Tried to fly. No go. He listened for any sounds of danger. The pounding of his heart almost took away his breath. Stay steady and keep moving. A putrid smell. Rotting corpse? The scent of feces "Ouch!" Something was ripping out his hair. Blindly, he reached out. "Who's there?"

"The old man warned you." A hideous, hoarse whisper froze Tom in his tracks.

"Who are you?"

"He told you who I was."

"Hades?"

A screeching, ear-piercing laugh echoed through the tunnel. He revealed himself to Tom. His eyes were literally bleeding. The rest of him was just a dark red blob outlined. His head was half human, half goat. He had large ram horns and hairless wings, the chest and arms of a human, and the big legs of a goat.

"This tunnel belongs to me."

"I'm just traveling through; don't plan to stay."

Another hideous laugh. "Fool."

"I may be, but I will pass."

A deep, harsh croak rang out. Flapping wings fluttered around his head. "That's Raven giving you a message." Hades whispered.

"Why?"

"He's telling you to turn back."

"No way." Tom refused.

"Hoped you'd say that."

Three quick claps. Soft red light. There were images, but they were dark. A three-headed dog showed up. That of a lion, a goat, and a snake.

"Jesus! What the hell?"

"That's Cerberus. His job is to guard my tunnel. One simple rule. If you can calm him, you can pass by him. By the way, no one has ever succeeded… Well, except Hercules."

Tom extended his hand. He talked softly. "Calm down. Calm down. I'm not here to fight. Just want to pass."

The lion's head pounced, flashing its mammoth ivory teeth. Tom yanked his hand back. He felt for the flute Pat had given him. He began to play. Played beautifully. Cerberus listened. The beast struggled to stay awake. Finally, he fell into a deep slumber.

Hades watched. "How did you know that song?"

"I don't know. Don't even know what it's called."

"You're a smart one. 'Dance of the Blessed Spirits' calms Cerberus. Puts him to sleep."

"You said I could pass."

"Don't toy with me. What's your name?"

"Tom… Tom Hunt."

"What's driving you into this horrid tunnel?"

"Don't know, do you?"

"Ah, smart-ass, are ya? That's all right. But I know you're doing it for love. Enjoy this…"

Detailed images of Cabot and Tara wrapped in pure pleasure. Their pelvises exploded together with red energy. "You'll never give her the pleasure that Cabot does."

"You bastard, I know that's not true."

"She doesn't want you to find her. She doesn't miss you. You dreamed it all up, Tom."

"She's waiting for me."

"Ooooh, no, no, no, Tom. She's committed to Cabot, not to you."

"You're lying."

"You deny what you see? Want to see it again? Perhaps more detail?"

"You made a bad mistake, Hades."

"How… how so?"

"Their lovemaking would have been a dance of love and communication. All of their chakras would have been lit up, not just their sacral chakra."

"What? I've shown you them in love."

"Yes, you did. But that was an ugly trick."

Hade's piercing scream forced Tom to cover his ears. "Get thy behind me, Satan." Tom blurted out the bible. Standing tall, he put his hands down and began to walk forward.

"No…" The last sound Tom was able to hear trailed off behind him as he left the tunnel.

Fresh air and beautiful mountains were there outside the tunnel. He had an adrenaline rush. He was tripping his ass off more than ever now. *I wonder if I will get any higher?*

A strong force pulled him backward. His silver cord. His thread of energy tying his body to his soul. Being used to drag him back toward the tunnel. Tom grabbed a tree and held on for dear life. He dug his toes into the snow. His arms trembled. His hands were cramped. Screaming pain. He let go.

"No one gets through my tunnel," screamed Hades.

Tom grabbed onto a large rock. He reached out for a weapon. Anything. He held onto the big rock while feeling the dirt with his other. At last, a rock with a sharp edge. Time to commit. Time to make a choice. His silver cord had become a nuisance. The sharp edge of the rock took care of that. The cord severed.

The tunnel began shaking violently and then burst into flames. A terrifying scream. Was Hades caught in the flames? Another scream. There's my answer. Tom stood and brushed himself off. His cord had disappeared. No sign of it had ever been there. His choice had been made.

The shaking of the tunnel began to creep down the hillside. Huge boulders shimmered down. Tom ran; he tried to fly. No way. He was in a different world. The stones missed his head, but they steadily pelted the back of his legs. Some missed his head by inches.

The steep path down challenged him. Faster to rowboat on his ass... Tom dove into a small gully.

Boulders were flying everywhere. The ground practically roared with sounds of thunder as it waved.

It happened so fast. And then it was gone. No more thunder. The landslide stopped. Up on the ridge, the tunnel had collapsed. Dirt and smoke were everywhere.

Chapter Thirty-Two
Green Mountains, Vermont
1975
Nowhere Man

Where's Pat? I'm fuckin' tripping my ass off! Is that smoke just over the next ridge? Do I smell rabbit stew? Fuckin' A. That's got to be Cabot's cabin. Just in time, too. The wind was howling, and it was so fucking cold. He wished Tara was here. He'd hold her so tightly.

Fuck! There is no cabin. No smoke. No stew. He stumbled around aimlessly. There were footprints. *Shit, those are mine.* He was lying in the snow, literally exhausted. Clouds floated by. As a kid, he would sit in the back seat of his parent's car and watch the clouds. *They were so high.* They were animals. Rabbits. Turtles. Even dragons. He ran on top of them.

An Emily Bronte poem was perfect for what he was seeing. It was the first poem that he memorized.

> The night is darkening round me,
> The wild winds coldly blow.
> But a tyrant spell has bound me
> And I cannot, cannot go.

The giant trees are bending
Their bare boughs weighed with snow.
The storm is fast descending,
And yet I cannot go.

Clouds beyond clouds above me,
Waste beyond wastes below;
But nothing drear can move me;
I will not, cannot go.

"Tom… Tom! Wake up! "

Pat shook him. A limp body… Shook him again. Brushed the snow from his face.

"Come back, Tom. Damn it, I'm so sorry. I had to go around the tunnel. It closed after you entered. Tom, I found them, Tom! They are looking for you. The cabin is just around the bend. Tara's calling for you. Can you hear her, Tom? It's your home. You made it!"

*

Hunters found Tom's frozen body. It leaned against an evergreen. His sleeping bag was wrapped around him. The coroner said he had starved to death.

His parents had him cremated as he had wished. They spread his ashes on the Appalachian Trail he loved so much. It happened on a brilliantly clear night in January. On the night of the Wolf Moon Rising.

Printed in the USA
CPSIA information can be obtained
at www.ICGtesting.com
LVHW041314051024
793003LV00002B/134